The Haunting Of
AVELINE JONES

For Alison, who loved spooky things.

First published in the UK in 2020 by Usborne Publishing Ltd., Usborne House,
83-85 Saffron Hill, London EC1N 8RT, England, usborne.com
Usborne Verlag, Usborne Publishing Ltd., Prüfeninger Str. 20, 93049 Regensburg,
Deutschland, VK Nr. 17560

Illustrations by Keith Robinson.

Cover typography by Sarah J Coleman/inkymole.com

A CIP catalogue record for this book is available from the British Library.

JFMAMJJA OND/22 ISBN 9781474972147 05657/7

Printed and bound in Great Britain by CPI Group (UK) Ltd, Croydon, CR0 4YY

The Haunting Of AVELINE JONES

Phil Hickes

Illustrated by Keith Robinson

USBORNE

"I live in a place where it's always dark
and the wind never stops blowing."
P.P.

Chapter 1

A Chill in the Air

It had been the coldest October for years. Nobody could escape the wind's icy breath, which somehow managed to squeeze through even the thickest of scarves. Puddles froze. Pipes burst. People wobbled around on frosty pavements with their arms stuck out as if pretending to be aeroplanes. Schools closed early for half-term and children cheered.

Aveline Jones sat in her mum's car and heaved a sigh that said more about her melancholy mood than words ever could. While a few days off school would normally have been cause for a major celebration, her plans for doing a lot of *not-a-lot* had been scuppered. And now fate was taking her to a different place altogether. A place that threatened to be even colder than the frozen city she'd left behind.

Malmouth.

Her mum had told her that it could get bitterly cold by the sea, and Aunt Lilian's house was apparently so close to the shore that the windows were crusted with salt. The thought made Aveline wince. That's why her suitcase groaned under the weight of scarves, coats, bobble hats, woolly jumpers, thermal fleeces, thick socks, boots and gloves. She'd even brought her zebra onesie, which didn't normally make an appearance until December.

Aveline stared gloomily out of the car window as the countryside passed by in a bleak blur. They must be getting close to Malmouth by now, she thought, though seeing the weary expression on her mum's face, she resisted the temptation to ask how much further they had to go.

The journey down from Bristol had been long and miserable. Aveline had tried listening to her music for a while, but the songs sounded forced and out-of-place on such a dreary day and so she'd given up. The countryside appeared to have given up, too. With most of their leaves having been blown away, the trees resembled plucked chickens, their trunks black and shiny with slime.

The skinny hedgerows
looked similarly
hungry and ill,
all the colour
having been sucked
out of them by the
vampire weather.
The only living things to
be seen were the rooks that
sat hunched in the branches, hurling their angry curses
across the empty countryside.

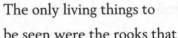

"I saw the sea, the sea saw me, I saw it first, tee-hee-hee," Aveline's mum said, in a voice that sounded like laughing was the last thing on her mind.

Aveline turned to squint between the manic windscreen wipers. Barely visible on the horizon stretched a thin greyish-blue band of ocean, the wind slicing the tops off the waves as if they were boiled eggs.

"Is that Malmouth?"

"Certainly is. Won't take long now."

Snakes wriggled in Aveline's stomach. Her mum was off to visit Aveline's granny, who lay ill in a hospital in Scotland. The trip would be too far and too upsetting for Aveline, her mum had decided, and so Aunt Lilian had offered to put Aveline up over half-term until her mum returned.

Aunt Lilian remained something of a puzzle. Nice but cold, like ice cream. She'd been a teacher at a posh boarding school but had moved to the Cornish coast a few months ago to work as a private tutor. Aveline hadn't spent much time with her aunt before now, mainly because Aunt Lilian used to live in Scotland, too, which was a little far away for regular visits. But on the few occasions she'd met her, Aveline always felt a little intimidated. Her aunt ran her life – and house – in the manner of a boot camp, where the "do not"s far outnumbered the "do"s. Sometimes Aveline wondered if her aunt wouldn't be better employed as a prison guard. Now she faced the daunting prospect of being alone with her until early November.

The thought gave her the chills.

Like many coastal towns, Malmouth's streets were narrow and winding, so that every time a car came in the opposite direction, they were forced to slow almost to a complete stop before inching carefully past.

"It's a bit empty, isn't it?" Aveline said, as they began the steep descent into the town.

"Well, we are in the middle of a terrible cold spell,

love," her mum said, nudging the car forward. "All these places along the coast tend to quieten down once the tourists leave. Don't worry, I'm sure there'll still be lots to do."

Despite it being only late afternoon, the sky looked ominously dark. Back home, the city centre where Aveline met her friends would still be teeming with shoppers. Here, the streets were practically deserted. They drove past terraced houses in silence, the town's desolate atmosphere creeping into the car. An old man walking his dog stopped to glare at them as they passed, an annoyed scowl on his face, almost as if their car had *HELLO, WE'RE STRANGERS* spray-painted on the side.

"I wonder…if Malmouth has any ghosts?" Aveline said, doing her best to sound casual.

Her mum sighed.

"Aveline, we've barely arrived and you're already talking about ghosts?"

"But it looks creepy."

"Everywhere looks creepy if all you ever read about is ghosts. Honestly, Aveline, I do wish you'd broaden your interests a little more, because all you're going to do is give yourself nightmares."

They'd had the same conversation many times before

and Aveline knew her mum thought her tastes very odd, but she couldn't help it. Ever since she'd found a book about ghosts in her local library, she'd been fascinated by the idea of people coming back after they died. Over time it had morphed into something of an obsession. After all, if the books were to be believed then England was jam-packed with spooky beings: headless horsemen, ladies in grey, spectral monks and nuns, demon dogs with blazing red eyes and slavering jowls – they were everywhere. So Aveline always kept an eye out, just in case.

And Malmouth appeared to have all the right ingredients for a haunting. Stormy weather. Old houses. The eerie grey swell of the sea. But, most of all, that uncanny emptiness that ghosts liked best. She was sure that was why they were always found on windswept moors, in ruined abbeys and crumbling castles. But for the sake of keeping the peace, Aveline decided to keep her thoughts to herself – and her eyes peeled.

Moments later, they emerged into the centre of the town. Twinkling lights outside The George Hotel added some cheer, though Aveline couldn't help but notice that inside a bored-looking barman watched the flat-screen TV on his own. The fish-and-chip shop was doing marginally better business, although there were still more seagulls than customers. A boy with floppy black hair sat on a bench outside, reading a book with one hand while using the other to stuff his mouth with chips. Glancing up, he noticed Aveline looking at him and paused, one chip held halfway to his mouth. Reddening, Aveline quickly glanced away. At least now she knew there was one other person her own age in the town.

"Here we go, Lilian lives just along here," Aveline's mum said, swinging the car around a roundabout and onto a road that ran parallel to the beach.

To their left, waves crashed down onto the pebbled beach in angry explosions of foam. A little further on, the concrete harbour wall curved out into the sea like a giant stone tentacle, beside which anchored fishing boats bobbed around in the sheltered bay. To their right ran a line of cosy-looking fishing cottages, all painted different pastel colours. Many were decorated with bunches of antique buoys, hung on the gates and doorways like giant plastic grapes. The windows glowed a welcoming orange and gold and, for the first time since setting off, Aveline wondered if Malmouth might turn out to be better than she'd expected.

Up ahead, outside the cottage at the end of the row, somebody watched them approach. It appeared to be another boy. He leaned against the garden wall at an awkward angle, as if he'd fallen against it but was unable to pull himself back up. He was odd-looking – his skin appeared too pale, his hair too dry and frizzy, a combination that suggested he might be suffering from some dreadful sickness.

"Is he okay, do you think?" Aveline's mum said.

Aveline didn't reply. She sensed something wasn't quite right, the back of her neck growing cold. It was a feeling she got sometimes, when she walked past abandoned houses with boarded-up windows or lay in bed at night reading something spooky. It told her that all was not well. That perhaps, somewhere in the shadows, something otherworldly lurked.

As they drew closer, the boy still hadn't moved. Their car slowed. Like a pair of inquisitive owls, the two of them turned their heads to peer at the strangely rigid figure.

Dead eyes stared back at them.

A clown mouth curved upwards in a cruel smirk.

The figure's head was made from a grubby white buoy, with eyes, nose and mouth scrawled on in blood-red paint. Its limbs were stiff because they'd been pulled from an old shop-dummy. It wore a black woollen hat on top of a garish ginger wig and had been dressed in charity-shop clothes – a tatty oversized jacket hung past its knees, underneath which were paint-splattered trousers.

Aveline screwed up her face.

"Ugh, I can't believe we thought that was real. What's it supposed to be?"

Her mum shrugged her shoulders. "Some kind of Halloween decoration, I suppose, but I certainly wouldn't want one in *my* garden. It'd give me the creeps."

Mystery solved, they drove on, though Aveline couldn't help but stare back over her shoulder at the awful dummy. Maybe it'd been made for some local competition. If that was the case, Aveline doubted it would win any prizes. Unless they had one for Ugliest Scarecrow Ever.

Aunt Lilian's house lay a little further on, one street back from the seafront. The house was pretty old by the looks of it, but had been modernized in places, giving it a curious blend of old and new. Its walls were whitewashed and the window frames were ocean-blue, although the paint had faded and peeled. Smoke curled out of the chimney before being snatched away by the wind. A small dog yapped angrily at them through a gap between the curtains.

They knocked on the door. A few seconds later Aunt Lilian opened it, her silhouette a black cross in the doorway. Behind her legs, the terrier dog continued to bark.

"Oh, do be quiet, Charlie, they come in peace," Aunt Lilian hissed at the dog. "I was wondering what had happened to you two. Didn't we agree you'd be here by three?" she said, glancing at her watch to emphasize the inconvenience.

Aveline felt like she was late for class.

"Sorry, Lilian, we got caught up in some roadworks outside Bristol," Aveline's mum explained. "And the weather didn't help much, you know how the rain slows everything down."

The two sisters embraced, similar in looks but not in physique – Aunt Lilian all bones and hard edges with her hair yanked back from her face into a tight bun, while Aveline's mum was softer, her hair falling in bouncy curls. Hard and soft. Much like their characters, Aveline thought, wondering how the two of them managed to be both alike and unalike all at once.

"Ah, Aveline, how are you?" Aunt Lilian said.

"Fine, thanks," Aveline mumbled.

"Well? Come and give me a hug."

It was like wrapping her arms around one of the trees she'd seen on the journey down, all twigs and knots. Then Aunt Lilian held her out at arm's length and studied her, squeezing her shoulders as if Aveline were a grapefruit in the supermarket.

"You've grown," Aunt Lilian said.

Aveline wasn't sure if that was true. Still one of the shortest in her class, she felt like a garden gnome compared to some of her taller, more athletic classmates. But she still liked hearing Aunt Lilian say it. That was another of her aunt's unusual characteristics, Aveline decided. With just a few words she could either make you feel on top of the world, or like something she'd found stuck to the bottom of her shoe.

"Hurry up and bring your things in then, it's not a day to be leaving the door open."

The air smelled fresh and briny. They unpacked the car to the sound of gulls crying and waves crashing, before making their way into Aunt Lilian's home. The kitchen had a flagstone floor with a large Aga oven dominating the room. Charlie's basket lay in front of it and, having satisfied himself that Aveline and her mum didn't work for the Post Office, he settled down in it. The kitchen led through into the living room, which reflected Aunt

Lilian's abnormally tidy approach to home decor, looking as though everything from the lamps to the cushions on the sofa had been lined up with a measuring tape.

Aunt Lilian led the way upstairs, her long, thin body casting strange shadows on the white plaster walls. Behind her, Aveline hauled her bulging suitcase up the narrow stairs.

"Your first time here, isn't it?"

"Yes."

"Well, you should know that the cottage was built sometime in the late eighteenth century," Aunt Lilian said, sounding like a tour guide taking visitors around a medieval castle. "And because of its age there are a few quirks you'll need to get used to, one of which is the heating. It can be very unpredictable, so I've put an electric heater in your room in case you get cold, though please use it sparingly. Blankets are, of course, the more cost-effective option, and you'll find plenty of them in the wardrobe. I'll leave you to unpack – socks and underwear go in the top drawer, tops in the middle and bottoms in the bottom. All outerwear and footwear goes in the wardrobe, though dirty shoes and boots are to be left at the kitchen door. Come down when you're ready."

Aveline was tempted to ask what time morning inspection would begin but held her tongue. While she'd known her aunt was strict, she couldn't believe that she'd already been given instructions on how to unpack, but she dutifully sorted her clothes into the correct drawers. What an odd beginning to her seaside visit, Aveline thought. She wasn't sure if she would be able to stand being ordered around for the next few days.

Resisting the urge to scream "Help!" out of the bedroom window, she joined her mum and aunt downstairs. They ate some lasagne that Aunt Lilian served in mathematically exact chunks, before settling down in the front room. As the two sisters caught up on their news, and with no TV or internet to entertain herself, Aveline attempted to text a friend, but the signal was so weak that she gave up. She did notice with some relief that Aunt Lilian had a computer set up on a desk at the back of the living room. Aveline wouldn't have been surprised if her aunt still communicated via telegram. Time dragged and Aveline found herself yawning uncontrollably. Tomorrow, she would have to find herself something to do, otherwise she'd go mad.

"I see the sea air's got to you, Aveline," her aunt said. "Better than hot chocolate or camomile tea. Do you know, since I moved here, I've never had a bad night's sleep? I don't know how you manage to get any rest in that noisy city with the traffic roaring about all hours of the night."

Behind Aunt Lilian's back, Aveline's mum rolled her eyes. Aveline grinned, although it reminded her that tomorrow her mum would be setting off to see Granny and she'd be left here on her own.

"Okay, I'm off to bed, night then," Aveline said, deciding that if she was going to be doing nothing, then she might as well be doing nothing in a warm bed.

"Goodnight, Aveline," Aunt Lilian said, before adding, "Oh, and don't worry if you hear any strange noises in the night, it's just the old house being cranky."

"Or it might be me snoring," Aveline's mum said. "Bedtime for me, too, Lilian, I'm having trouble keeping my eyes open."

"I'll make up a bed for you down here in front of the fire," Aunt Lilian said.

"Night, Mum," Aveline said.

"Night, love, see you in the morning before I leave."

Before I leave.

Aveline trudged upstairs, suddenly feeling very alone. Outside the wind keened, the little house trembling beneath its gusts. Aveline brushed her teeth quickly, the bathroom approximately the same temperature as an igloo, before scuttling across the landing and into her bedroom. Jumping into bed, she wrapped the sheets and blankets tightly around her and closed her eyes.

Despite what Aunt Lilian said, Aveline found it much noisier by the coast. While it was true that back home in Bristol you could hear the traffic at night, she found that oddly comforting – simply people going about their business. Here it was different. The crashing waves. The howling winds. Salt water spitting at the windows. No human noises at all and everything so wild. It made her feel very small and vulnerable.

Just as she was nodding off, Aveline heard laughter. A mocking, childlike chortle, far off in the night. Raising her head off the pillow, she strained to listen, remembering the creepy scarecrow they'd seen in the garden. What if it came alive at midnight? Was it dragging itself towards the house at this very moment? She hadn't forgotten the eerie sensation that had rippled through her earlier, but told herself she was just being stupid. Her mum already thought she read too many scary books. Besides, scarecrows didn't really come alive. Nothing could hurt her. She was safe.

Shivering, she lay back down and pulled the covers up as far as they could go without actually covering her head. *Silly.*

Probably just a seagull, or some squeaky pipes – her aunt had warned her.

Then sleep washed over her, like a wave drifting up over the pebbles.

"It's weird. Nobody seems to go out in the evening here. Not once the sun goes down."
P.P.

Chapter 2

The Book Boy

In the morning, Aveline said goodbye to her mum.

"Don't worry, I'll be back to rescue you soon," her mum whispered in her ear before giving her a big hug.

Aveline clung to her mum for a moment before letting her go, aware that Aunt Lilian watched their farewell with narrowed eyes. She didn't want her aunt to know that she was secretly dreading the next few days. Being in this quirky old house with all its rules felt like stepping back in time, and although she and her aunt were family, it had never been just the two of them alone before. It felt awkward and claustrophobic. Also, it seemed Aveline's entertainment options were going to be very limited. Aunt Lilian had explained, with something of a triumphant note in her voice, how mobile phone reception on the coast was intermittent, which Aveline wished she'd known before so she could have brought some books. Of course she could use the computer, but only for half an hour each day. Any longer than that wasn't healthy, Aunt Lilian had said, in a manner that suggested the internet wasn't something she approved of either.

"I'm going into town this morning, perhaps you'd like to come with me and explore a little?" Aunt Lilian suggested after Aveline's mum had driven off. "There's a small bookshop you might find interesting, although the owner does have a tendency to talk too much. We could meet for a coffee afterwards if you'd like?"

It sounded like an okay idea and at least it might help to pass the time. Besides, Aveline sensed that this was Aunt Lilian making an effort to be nice.

As they stepped outside, the wind hit Aveline like a slap, forcing tears from her eyes and making her bend double. Despite her rangy, thin frame, Aunt Lilian seemed impervious to it, and marched along purposefully. Beside them, grey waves ebbed and flowed, adding even more stormy energy to the day.

"Here we are," Aunt Lilian said a few minutes later, coming to a halt outside what appeared to be someone's front door. Aveline's confusion must have been apparent, because Aunt Lilian sighed and pointed down some steps to the basement, where a faded wooden sign swayed in the wind.

Lieberman's Second-Hand Books

It was unlike any bookshop Aveline had ever seen. Its windows were thick with grime. The tiny doorway resembled the entrance to a hobbit hole. Water dripped from a broken drainpipe into a small puddle at the base of the steps. Yet there was something intriguing about it, too. A secret book cave waiting to be explored.

"Do you have a watch, Aveline?"

Aveline shook her head. "No, but I can check the time on this," she said, holding up her phone.

A look of mild distaste flashed across Aunt Lilian's face. "Very well. Come and meet me at 11.15. Walk up to the end of the street, turn right, and you'll see Brilliant Beans, the coffee shop, right opposite the hotel. Don't be late. Oh, and try not to get into a conversation with Mr Lieberman or you'll be there all day."

With that, Aunt Lilian strode away.

Aveline made her way down the steps and pushed the

door open. A bell tinkled as she entered. She liked that. It sounded old-fashioned and sweet. If she ever became Prime Minister, all doors would have little bells.

Inside, it was clear that the bookshop wouldn't be running out of stock any time soon. A large table dominated the centre, on top of which tottering piles of books threatened to collapse at any minute. Surrounding it, shelves were loaded to breaking point with *more* books. The space was small and deliciously gloomy, with dust motes floating like golden fairies and the musty aroma of aged paper hanging heavy in the air. This was Aveline's sort of place. And chances were, it would have her sort of books.

Aveline started as a white-haired old man popped up from beneath the counter.

"Don't tell me," he said, his voice creaking like an oak tree in the wind. "Horses."

"I'm sorry?" Aveline said.

"Horses," he said again. "You're looking for a book about horses. I like to think I have a talent for matching people to books and I see something equine in you that leads me to immediately think of horses. I have a copy of *Black Beauty* somewhere, in excellent condition. I can let you have it for a very good price."

"Um, no thanks," Aveline said, holding a hand to her mouth to hide her smile. He couldn't have been more wrong and yet she didn't want to tell him just yet. He seemed to be enjoying himself too much.

"No to horses, eh? Okay, well, let me think for a minute. Hmm…"

The old man narrowed his eyes and stared intently at Aveline. He stood so tall and thin he reminded her of a plant that had outgrown its pot. Twisting the tassels on her scarf between her fingers, she waited for him to guess again.

"Ach, I have it!" he cried, thumping the counter and sending up a cloud of dust. "You're an explorer! That's what brought you to my shop no doubt, a nose for adventure! Tell me, have you ever read *Around The World In Eighty Days*? I have a hardback copy with some fine illustrations, I can let you have it for next to nothing."

"Um, maybe," Aveline said. She didn't want to hurt the old man's feelings, but when it came to reading she had *very* specific interests. Inhaling the giddy smell of a thousand books, she took a long look around the shop. "Do you have any books about ghosts?"

The countertop received another thump.

"Ghosts! Ach, of course! I was just about to say that,"

he said. "Of course I do. I have hundreds of them. I have books about every subject under the sun. Or in this case, perhaps I should say *under the moon*? The witching hour, eh, and things that go bump in the night?"

Aveline nodded eagerly. Malmouth had already begun to feel a bit creepy. Some research into its supernatural background could be very useful. If she was going to meet any ghosts, it was best to be prepared.

"My name's Ernst, by the way. Ernst Lieberman, owner of this humble enterprise. And you?"

"Aveline Jones."

"An excellent name," Mr Lieberman said. "You see, in my book, anyone who *likes books* is excellent, too. So, Aveline, take a look around and you'll see books that are crying out for a little love. All are welcome here, you see. Nobody is ever turned away. Even if someone brings me a book about something very dull and boring, like how conveyor belts are built, I welcome them all the same, because books are the most precious thing in all the world, don't you think?" Pausing, he frowned at her. "You're not interested in how conveyor belts are built, by any chance?"

Aveline laughed and shook her head. Aunt Lilian had been right about him talking a lot, but she liked listening to him. He resembled the shop in a way, all old and creased and ramshackle.

"My father brought me to this country when I was a small boy," Mr Lieberman continued. "He told me that back in Germany there were people who used to burn books, which is just about the worst thing anyone can do. So he made me promise to look after *my books* as if they were my children. So here I am, a father with a million little paper children! Maybe today you'll adopt one of them?"

"Maybe," Aveline said. "I hope so."

The old man rested his pointy chin on one hand. "Well then I suppose you'd better step this way. I keep all our ghost books at the back, where it's dark and a little bit creepy. They prefer it that way."

The old man turned and shouted. "Harold! We have a very important customer, please come and lend us your assistance!" Turning back to Aveline, the old man smiled. "Harold is my great-nephew, by which I mean he is the son of *my* nephew, not a *great* nephew, although he most certainly is *great*, too." The old man checked he was still alone before adding in a low voice, "Though you may find him a tad aloof. He's a bit shy – I'm sure you understand."

Aveline adopted her most serious expression and

nodded. Actually, she did know what it felt like to be shy – like right now, standing in a cramped little bookshop, about to be introduced to a total stranger.

A tall boy stepped into the doorway behind the old man.

"Ah, there you are. Harold, this is Aveline, a very important customer."

The boy glanced in her direction but didn't say anything. Aveline wondered if maybe that was because Mr Lieberman did all the talking for the both of them. She could see the family resemblance though. Tall and thin like his great-uncle, Harold had a long black fringe which fell down over his face, through which he stared out dolefully, as if he resented being summoned to assist customers.

Then the realization struck her.

It was him.

Book Boy.

The same boy she'd seen stuffing his face outside the fish-and-chip shop.

"Harold, I wonder could you show Aveline where our ghost books are kept, please?"

Harold lingered for only a second before replying, but to Aveline it felt like the longest second ever.

"They're up here," he grunted. "Follow me."

She would have been happier if Harold had just pointed her in the right direction and left her to it, though when she followed him up the small flight of stairs, she realized why she hadn't been left to her own devices.

The back room appeared even more jumbled than the front. Half library, half storage room, cardboard boxes full of books competed for space with the overflowing shelves. She could have been wandering around up here for years. It was even gloomier than the main room, too. Harold clicked an antique lamp on, probably just for her benefit, as he seemed to glide through the jumble of books as if well used to its chaos.

Bending down in front of one of the shelves, Harold swept his fringe aside with a carefully practised toss of his head.

"This place is a right tip, but I think this is where he keeps them."

Aveline actually quite liked the chaotic little bookshop, but she kept her opinion to herself. Now she had more important business to attend to. Seeing the little bowed shelf with the label *Hauntings & Apparitions*, she had to resist the urge to push Harold aside. It was like finding hidden treasure.

"Thanks," Aveline said.

"S'alright," Harold grunted again.

"Do you work here then?" Aveline said, feeling it only polite to make a little conversation.

"On the weekends." Harold sniffed. "My mum and dad go away a lot with their jobs, so my great-uncle looks after me while they're gone. It's not really work though. Most of the time I just sit in the back and read books."

"That sounds great," Aveline said, feeling a little jealous. She'd love to have somewhere like this to call her own. "By the way, I think I saw you yesterday, as we were driving through town. You were reading a book and eating chips."

"Oh...yeah...probably," Harold said, before lapsing into silence.

There was an awkward pause. Aveline wondered if she should try again, but Harold wasn't making this easy. Just as she felt herself redden, Harold pointed down at the bottom shelf.

"Why do you like all this ghost stuff anyway?"

She hadn't been expecting that *particular* question and it threw her off balance.

"Um, I don't know," she said, twisting her fingers in her scarf. "I suppose I like scaring myself. And I've always wondered if ghosts are real or not. I think there must be something in it though. They can't *all* be imaginary. Do you believe in them?"

Harold snorted. "Nah, load of rubbish, I reckon. Anyway, if you like ghosts you've come to the right place. This town is like a graveyard."

"Yeah, I saw a scarecrow that looked pretty creepy."

"Wait until you've met some of the locals, they're even scarier."

Aveline giggled. "It can't be that bad here."

"Nah, it's alright really. Just a bit on the quiet side. Good chips though. You'll have to come down and try them one night."

Aveline flushed again. "Okay."

"You here with your parents then?"

"My mum brought me down," Aveline said. "My dad lives in America. They divorced when I was young," she added. She always felt obliged to explain why her mum and dad lived thousands of miles apart. "But I'm actually staying with my Aunt Lilian."

"Oh. Okay. Well anyway, I'll leave you to it."

"Thanks."

Aveline thought she saw a hint of a blush on Harold's face as he slunk away, but it was hard to tell with all that hair. At least now she could discover what delights Mr Lieberman had hidden away in this dark and dusty corner.

With Harold's departure the room grew silent. Aveline imagined the books all holding their breath, waiting to see if she'd pick them. The way Mr Lieberman spoke about them as lonely people made her a little sad that she couldn't take them all home. Dropping to her knees, she angled her head and let her eyes rove greedily across the spines. Most of them were old. Very old. Dotted here and there were a few paperbacks that had seen better days, but by and large the books were of a style that had disappeared long ago – thick books with ridged spines and faded covers that were probably once brightly coloured, but had dulled with age and the touch of a hundred eager fingers. Inside, the type was old-fashioned and small, much smaller than she was used to. The edges of the pages were tinged with ochre. In much the same way that an old person's skin wrinkles and dulls, so too had the pages of these books.

Aveline sighed with pleasure. It seemed fitting that these ghostly books were a little decrepit.

But now she needed to decide what to buy. Her mum had left her some spending money. She needed to make it last, but a second-hand book wouldn't break the bank. Glancing at her phone, she saw that she had thirty minutes or so before she was due to meet her aunt at the coffee shop. Biting her bottom lip, Aveline began pulling books from the shelf.

Collected Ghost Stories.
Best Ghost Stories.
Tales of Terror.
Encyclopaedia of Witchcraft & Magic.
Tales of the Supernatural.
Haunted Britain.

On and on the titles went, and Aveline didn't own a single one. In just a few minutes she'd put aside an impressive pile of possible purchases. Deciding which one to actually buy would be an impossible task.

But then one book in particular caught her eye. Bottle-green with gold lettering, it looked as if it belonged in a museum or university library. Also, unlike the other books, this one was actually about the area around Malmouth.

Ghosts and Phantoms of Dorset, Devon and Cornwall.

Exactly what she'd been looking for.

Pulling it out, Aveline opened it at random and began to read. The excerpt she landed upon concerned a mythical creature known as a *Bucca*, or *Knocker*, so called because they lived deep in the Cornish tin mines and *knocked* on the walls of the caves to tell the miners when the tunnels were about to collapse. Aveline tried to imagine what it would be like to be deep underground in the dark, only to hear a tapping that told you there were just seconds to escape. Reading on, it appeared that the miners were split about whether the creatures were good or evil, with some believing that—

"Boo!"

Aveline jumped. Scowling, she pushed up her glasses and saw Harold standing over her with a sly grin. He moved as quietly as a cat stalking a starling.

"Seen any ghosts yet then?"

"No, I think you scared them away," Aveline retorted, deciding at that moment that she much preferred the great-uncle to the great-nephew. She held up the book she'd been reading. "I have to go and meet my aunt. How much is this one?"

Flipping his hair back, Harold frowned at the book.

"No idea. None of them have any price tags, but my

uncle seems to know how much everything is. Give it here and I'll go ask him."

Reluctantly, Aveline handed the book over. It already felt like hers.

Following Harold back into the front room of the shop, Aveline watched nervously as he passed the book to his uncle.

"She wants to know how much this one is."

"*Aveline* would like to know," his uncle corrected him.

"Yeah."

Mr Lieberman pulled out a pair of half-moon spectacles and popped them on the bridge of his large nose. Squinting at the spine, he hummed tunelessly under his breath.

"Ah, now this one is actually very rare. It's been out of print for many years and I'd be surprised if there were another one in the whole country. Maybe there isn't? Ach, imagine that, owning the only copy!"

Aveline's eyes widened. Handing her the book, Mr Lieberman took off his spectacles and beamed at her.

"It's yours for one pound."

"Really? I mean, is that all?" Aveline said. She had a feeling the true price should be far higher. She glanced at Harold but he simply shrugged his shoulders as if this was all perfectly normal.

"Positive," Mr Lieberman said. "I can remember the price of every book in this shop and that one is one pound exactly. Do you wish to buy it?"

Aveline whipped a ten-pound note from her pocket and gleefully held it up. "Yes please."

"Excellent!" Mr Lieberman said. "Another book finds a welcoming home. Harold, please be so kind as to fetch Aveline some change, would you?"

Harold rang the sale up on the till before placing the book in a brown paper bag. "Here you go."

"Thanks," Aveline said.

"Sorry if I made you jump earlier."

"You didn't," Aveline said, not wanting Harold to think he'd got one over on her. "Though it is a little spooky back there."

"Everywhere in Malmouth is the same," Harold said with a grin. "Don't worry, you'll get used to it."

Mr Lieberman held out his knobbly hand for her to shake.

"Pleasure doing business with you, Aveline." Pausing, he placed a bony finger against his cheek. "You know, now I come to think of it, I seem to remember something about that book...what is it now?"

But Aveline couldn't wait any longer. Not if she wanted to stay on good terms with her aunt.

"I'm sorry, I really have to go. Bye – and thanks so much!"

The bell above the door tinkled a cheery farewell as she left.

"Oh my…oh dear," Mr Lieberman muttered to himself. "I remember now."

The old man's face had turned as white as a barn owl's.

"Last night I woke up and thought I saw
somebody standing in the corner of my bedroom,
but when I looked again they were gone."
P.P.

Chapter 3

The Missing Story

Aveline pushed open the door to the coffee shop. Luckily, she saw her aunt straight away, perched awkwardly on the edge of a leather sofa with a plate of untouched carrot cake in front of her.

"You're late," her aunt said. "Let me guess, the old man gave you a lecture on books?"

Aveline grinned sheepishly.

"I swear, if there was an Olympic event for talking, that man would win a gold medal," her aunt said, pausing to prod at the cake with her fork. "So, tell me, did you actually manage to find time to buy a book or did he just talk you to death?"

"No, I found one. An old one. Mr Lieberman said it's

very rare and probably the only copy in the whole country – and he only charged me a pound, too."

"Hmm, the only copy indeed. Sounds like our Mr Lieberman is a very persuasive bookseller. Let me see."

Frowning, Aveline pulled the book out of the brown paper bag and passed it across the table. She believed Mr Lieberman even if her aunt didn't.

Aunt Lilian picked it up and idly flicked through the pages, raising her eyebrows in a spiny arch of either surprise or disapproval.

"Ghosts, well I never," she muttered under her breath. "I seem to remember your mother telling me something about your strange taste in books."

Turning to the inside cover, Aunt Lilian leaned forward with a frown.

"What is it, Aunt?"

"Oh, nothing, just…um…trying to see when it was first published." Clapping the book shut, Aunt Lilian slid it across the table. "Okay, we need to get going, Charlie will be wondering where we've got to. I'll get you a hot chocolate to go."

While her aunt waited at the counter, Aveline opened the book. Something about her aunt's reaction felt a little weird, as if she'd seen something that had given her a fright. But the only thing on the inside of the front cover was a handwritten name.

Primrose Penberthy.

Pulling the book closer to her face, Aveline peered suspiciously at the signature of the former owner. It appeared to belong to a young girl, as the letters were carefully traced out, unlike the confident swoops and swirls of adult signatures. Aveline wondered who she was. This girl had actually touched these pages at one point, been eager to read them, just like her. It was an odd feeling, as if she'd stepped back in time for a moment.

"Okay, we're all paid up, let's be off."

Aveline reluctantly followed her aunt to the door, casting a longing look back at the cake. Her aunt had barely touched it. Why was she suddenly in such a rush?

The storm pounced on them as soon as they set foot outside. A rumble of thunder rippled across the sky, like the growl of a giant hound. Instinctively, they hunched their shoulders as bloated raindrops began to explode all around them. As they passed Lieberman's Books, the door opened and Mr Lieberman gesticulated at them.

"Ignore him, or we'll never get home," Aunt Lilian

ordered, walking so fast that Aveline had to jog to keep up.

Guiltily, Aveline glanced back and waved. Mr Lieberman appeared to say something, but in the roar of the storm he resembled a goldfish, his mouth opening and closing without any sound coming out. As it became clear they weren't stopping, his hands dropped to his sides and he watched them go with what Aveline thought was a rather concerned expression.

As they emerged onto the beach road, seagulls swooped through the air, surrendering to the strong gusts that tossed them about as they cried their mournful songs. Waves crashed up over the harbour wall like watery bombs. At times like this, Aveline felt very vulnerable, as if at any moment she might get lifted up by the wind, too, and hurled hundreds of miles away. For the second time that day she wished her mum hadn't gone.

"I hope there aren't any fishing boats out there," Aunt Lilian said, shouting to make herself heard.

Aveline held up a hand to shield her eyes and looked out across the water. White tops stretched to the horizon. Grey walls of water swayed and swelled, marching ominously towards the shore where they crashed onto the pebbles. Thankfully, the only boats she could see were anchored safely, the fury of the storm unable to break through the thick concrete wall behind which they cowered.

Reaching home in record time, the two of them burst through the door to be greeted by a delirious Charlie, whose usual suspicion had been replaced by an ecstatic delight. Aunt Lilian fetched them some towels to dry themselves. But Aveline didn't have time to be sitting around.

Not when there was a book waiting to be read.

Running straight up to her bedroom, she leaped headlong onto the bed with her precious bargain in both hands. Opening the front cover, she ran her hand over the signature inside. Did Primrose feel the same excitement when she'd first held this book? Maybe she'd also lain on her bed, hiding away in her own little private world.

Turning to the title page, Aveline had a look at the contents.

1. The Legend of Blackmarsh Cove.
2. The Phantom Coach.
3. Spirits of the Smuggler's Inn.
4. The Haunted Tin Mines.
5. The Beast of Bodmin.

6. The Ghost Bells of Boscastle.
7. Cornish Piskies.
8. The Lady in the Waves.

The titles gave her the chills. And with the rain hammering on the window, and the roar of the waves outside, it seemed the perfect day to stay indoors and read. Snuggling into her pillows, she started the story of Blackmarsh Cove, which interestingly, was actually on the same stretch of coastline as Malmouth.

The author explained that, like many secluded coves on the Cornish coastline, there had been a long history of piracy and smuggling around Blackmarsh Cove. It was concealed by rocky hills on all sides, which made it ideal for illicit trade, hidden as it was from prying eyes – especially those of the law. This particular legend concerned some smugglers who had arranged to be guided into shore at the cove one night by a colleague with a lantern. However, the man with the lantern had got drunk in the pub and forgotten and, as a result, the smugglers' ship had sailed into some rocks and sunk, with the loss of all on board. Ever since then, on cold, moonlit evenings, the ghosts of the smugglers would come ashore, searching for the man who'd betrayed them.

Aveline shivered. It was a good story. It made her glad she was safe indoors and not wandering lost on the coast. Harold, the book boy, had already told her that Malmouth was like a graveyard. Maybe he hadn't realized just how close he lived to a crew of phantom smugglers?

Quickly, she flicked through the rest of the book. But as she reached the last pages, a flush of anger spread across her face and up to her temples.

The final story didn't exist.

Each sentence of *The Lady in the Waves* had been deliberately crossed out, the culprit taking particular care to make sure the words couldn't be seen, sometimes with three or four strokes of the pen. It must have taken forever, which made the act feel all the more vindictive. How could anyone be so mean? What a horrible thing to do.

Aveline trailed a finger despondently over the pages as if she might magically restore the lost story.

Was it you, Primrose Penberthy?

Aveline considered her silent accusation. If it was Primrose, what would have made her want to do such a thing? It was maddening, to say the least. Like being given a gift you couldn't open or taking a mouthful of a delicious dinner before the plate is snatched away from under your nose. Maybe Mr Lieberman would know more about it? He seemed to have an encyclopaedic knowledge when it came to his books. At the very least he might know something about the previous owner. Turning back to the front of the book, Aveline read the name again, as if it might somehow offer up an answer.

She couldn't be certain the mysterious Primrose had done it. The story might have been crossed out long before the girl came across it.

Aveline walked to the window, lost in her thoughts. Outside, the storm flexed its muscles. Raindrops tinkled on the glass like tiny needles. Fountains of spray flew up over the sea wall in a spectacular display of ferocity. On the pebbled beach, a brave pair of dog walkers, clad in bright red anoraks, leaned into the wind as their saturated Labrador played tag with the rushing waves.

Beyond them, something caught Aveline's eye.

The back of her neck prickled.

Leaning forward, she hurriedly wiped the glass.

For a minute she thought she'd seen a small girl standing in the water. Aveline knew from personal experience how dangerous it was to go into the sea on a day like today. Two years ago, while holidaying in Pembrokeshire, her mum had had to run into the sea after a rip tide had dragged Aveline under the water. She remembered her blurred vision and the horrible sensation of salt water rushing into her nostrils. And that had been in the summer. She dreaded to think how cold the water would be now. Her mum had said that if you fell into a wintry sea, you only had a few minutes before hypothermia set in and you were done for.

But as she squinted through the squall, she noticed that the dog walkers hadn't reacted at all. They continued on their way as if nothing was amiss. They were so close to the shoreline it was impossible for them not to have noticed. Aveline rubbed at the misted window again, but all she could see now were crashing waves.

The rest of the day passed without incident. Aveline continued to think about the deleted story in her book. It felt unsettling, almost like a warning. As though someone had left her a message she couldn't read. The care that had been taken to make the final story unreadable didn't feel like the act of someone who was simply being malicious or mischievous, she now realized. In Aveline's opinion there could be no doubt: whoever had done it, they'd done it for a reason. Only she had no idea what that reason could be. The whole incident left her puzzled and, in truth, a little creeped out.

Once again the sea air worked its sleepy magic and, after a slightly awkward dinner with her aunt, Aveline excused herself early. For a while, she lay in bed listening to the sound of rain hammering against the windows and the wind whistling its mournful songs. Eventually she fell fast asleep—

—only to wake with a start.

Her bedside clock said 3.07 a.m. in glowing green. The storm must have passed, as all she could hear now was the *drip-drip-drip* of overflowing gutters and the suck and pull of the tide against the shingle.

Something else, too.

It sounded like a tiny spade being dragged across concrete.

A slow, deliberate scratching that made Aveline's breath catch in her throat, as if afraid to leave her nice warm body.

In an instant, her drowsiness melted away and she sat up in bed. The noise came from outside. Quickly, she began to run through a list of possible explanations. A dog. A cat. A bird. The heating coming on. Yet these all felt like poor excuses. Because, as she strained to listen, an image leaped into her mind and wouldn't go away.

Fingernails on glass.

What if somebody was downstairs, trying to get in through the kitchen window?

Leaping out of bed, Aveline ran into Aunt Lilian's room. Her aunt lay huddled underneath the bedclothes, snoring softly.

"Auntie, wake up," Aveline whispered. "I think someone's trying to break in."

Aunt Lilian hauled herself up onto one elbow and squinted at Aveline.

"What? We don't have any break-ins in Malmouth."

"I can hear scratching downstairs."

Yanking the bedclothes to one side, Aunt Lilian clambered out and together they walked onto the landing and down the stairs.

In the kitchen, Charlie stood in the middle of the flagstones, staring at the window, a low growl gurgling in his throat. His alertness set Aveline's nerves on edge, and she huddled a little closer to her aunt, who leaned over the sink to peer out of the window.

"Looks like I've found your burglar," Aunt Lilian said, extending a long accusing finger.

Aveline looked to where she pointed.

As the wind blew, it caused the branch of an ancient pear tree to bump against the window, causing a faint squeak.

"You weren't reading your *new* book by any chance, were you?" her aunt said, angling her eyebrows in judgement. "You know, the one about ghosts."

Aveline blushed. "It didn't sound like that from upstairs," she mumbled, embarrassed at having dragged her aunt out of bed in the middle of the night.

"Well, noises do often become distorted at night. Better safe than sorry, I suppose. Okay, back off to bed we go then. And don't have nightmares!"

Aveline was about to follow Aunt Lilian up, when she took one final look at the kitchen window. Something told her it would be wise to double-check. She might have an overactive imagination, but despite what her aunt said, the noises didn't quite match up.

She saw something on the window.

Smears on the glass.

Probably just needs a good clean, she thought to herself, suppressing a shudder.

But there was *something* about the tiny marks that appeared vaguely human.

Almost like a child's handprint.

"At night I think I hear footsteps, walking
slowly up and down outside my window,
but I daren't look out to see if anyone's there.
Probably just my imagination."
P.P.

Chapter 4

The Disappearance

The next day brought cold winds and dark skies but at least the rain had stopped. Aveline slept a little later than usual, the nocturnal incident having robbed her of a peaceful sleep. Even after returning to bed, she'd had trouble dozing off, the handprint on the window playing on her mind. At first, Malmouth had been something to laugh at. A quiet little seaside town with nothing much to do. But it had begun to unsettle her. The scarecrow. The unexplained noises. The sense that all was not right. Gazing out at the seafront in her dressing gown, Aveline felt homesick for the first time. The town had lost any sense of being cosy and quaint. It felt like somewhere that the world had forgotten about. As if she'd been forgotten, too.

Then she remembered the missing story in the book.

Over breakfast, she put it to her aunt.

"Aunt Lilian, would it be okay if I went down to the bookshop again?"

Aveline wanted to ask Mr Lieberman if he knew more about the final story in her book, or indeed anything about its previous owner. It seemed worth asking, even if that meant she was probably in for a long morning while she listened to everything he had to say (whether it was to do with the book or not). Part of her also wanted to see if Harold was still hanging around. By the sounds of it, he spent a lot of time with those books. He might know something, too.

"I don't see why not. I have a pupil coming for an English lesson, so it would actually be easier if you're out of the way," Aunt Lilian said with her customary bluntness. "Oh, by the way, your mother rang early this morning to say she arrived safely and everything's fine. I didn't want to wake you. Don't worry about calling her back as she'll probably be at the hospital with your granny."

Having negotiated an easier-than-expected escape, Aveline took a quick shower and dressed in her warm clothing. Then she placed the book carefully in her backpack. On her way out, she switched on the computer in the living room and wrote her mum a quick email, telling her she was sorry she'd missed her call, that she was bored but okay and that she hoped Granny felt better. As she was about to shut down the computer, she had a thought. Quickly, she tapped a name into the search bar.

Primrose Penberthy.

It took a moment or two for Aveline to get her head around what popped up on the screen.

THE DORSET TRIBUNE

POLICE STEP UP HUNT FOR MISSING SCHOOLGIRL

3rd November 1984

Police searching for an eleven-year-old girl missing from her home in Malmouth have today intensified their search in an effort to make a breakthrough. Primrose Penberthy was last seen by her parents around 9 p.m. on October 31st but disappeared sometime during the night. The family home reportedly showed no signs of forced entry and none of

Primrose's possessions had been taken. Her disappearance was described by one detective as "baffling".

Last night, police stopped pedestrians and drivers in the vicinity of Primrose's home, close to Malmouth harbour,

Primrose Penberthy

in the hope they may have seen something. Extensive searches have been made, including use of the force helicopter and canine units, with coastal search and rescue teams also called in to help. A team of volunteers has been assisting police with the search, scouring Malmouth and the surrounding area.

Detective Inspector Mike Farnham, who is leading the investigation, today made this appeal: "I would urge anyone with information relating to Primrose's disappearance to contact myself or any member of the investigating team. We're very concerned for Primrose's welfare and want to get her back to her family as soon as possible. We do know that Primrose is prone to sleepwalking, which is one line of enquiry we're pursuing, though we're keeping an open mind at this stage as to what may have happened."

Anyone with information can contact Malmouth Police Station directly.

A flush of fear and confusion warmed Aveline's cheeks. It had to be the same girl – how many Primrose Penberthys could there be?

So the girl who owned this book had gone missing from her home in Malmouth over thirty years ago. And not one of the links mentioned her having ever been found.

Aveline paused, her heart thumping in her chest. This book might even have been one of the last things Primrose touched before she disappeared. It felt like a thin gossamer strand had suddenly stretched out from the past to pull the two of them together. As if they now knew each other in some way, despite never having met. Grabbing the book from her backpack, Aveline opened the inside cover and ran her fingers over Primrose's signature, as if trying to gain a better understanding of who this girl was simply by the way she'd written her name. She felt seized by a strange impulse to find out more. Primrose's story had been forgotten, left to fade away into the past – just a sad column in an old newspaper.

Aveline was determined to change that and bring Primrose back into the present.

Pushing back her glasses, Aveline reread the article four or five times, before clicking on every other link that mentioned Primrose's disappearance. They all contained more or less the same information, which was fairly scant.

Primrose had disappeared into thin air.

Accompanying the reports was a grainy photograph of Primrose. It showed a girl with a scowl, a tiny downturned mouth, and a rather severe haircut. Despite the angry stare, Primrose looked pretty, Aveline thought, and also strangely familiar. Aveline wondered if they would have been friends. They had the same taste in books, after all. What on earth could have happened to her? People didn't just vanish.

Aveline noted that many of the sources mentioned that Primrose had been prone to sleepwalking, and it seemed to be the general consensus that she'd wandered off in her sleep and maybe fallen into the sea from the harbour wall. The theory offered a possible solution to the mystery, but there was no proof.

It seemed as though Primrose's disappearance would remain unsolved.

Unless…

She returned the book to her backpack and slung it

over her shoulder. As she opened the front door, the wind yanked it back out of her hand. Each gust felt like a handful of ice cubes, freezing any skin that wasn't protected. It made the walk to the bookshop that much quicker. This wasn't a day to be admiring the view. It was a day to tuck your head in and get to where you were going in the shortest possible time.

Walking quickly past the creepy child scarecrow, which still leered out at the world like an overgrown ventriloquist's puppet, Aveline hurried along the beach road. As she neared the end, something stopped her in her tracks. Her throat became dry. A gull cried out mockingly.

Haw! Haw!

The back of her neck felt as if someone had suddenly draped an icy-cold cloth across it. Because she could see another one.

Another child scarecrow.

It hadn't been there when they'd come back from town before. Aveline would have noticed for sure. It must have been put up sometime between yesterday evening and this morning.

This one was made of straw, lumpier and – on closer inspection – more hastily put together than its neighbour. It wore dungarees and a red-and-black striped jumper.

An old football had been used for a head, on which a pair of eyes had been scrawled in thick black pen, together with what might have been intended to be a goofy grin, but looked more like a grimace of pain. Aveline stopped to study the figure. For a second she thought she saw the curtains twitch in the cottage behind, but it could have been a trick of the light. The longer she stared at the scribbled face, the more it disturbed her. It seemed to hold her gaze, and she had a horrible feeling that as soon as she looked away, it would blink. It *must* be some sort of Halloween competition, she decided.

Forcing herself to walk away, she hurried along and reached Mr Lieberman's shop a few minutes later. As the door swung shut, and the bell stopped tinkling, the noise of the town and the sea fell away, to be replaced by a comforting silence and the strangely reassuring smell of dust and age. Behind the counter, Harold glanced up from his book and swept his fringe aside with one hand.

"Hello again," Aveline said, resisting the temptation to call him *Book Boy*. "Is your uncle around?"

"He's just popped out, but should be back in a minute," Harold said. "How's your ghost book? Sleeping with the lights on?"

"No, of course not," Aveline said scornfully, even

though she knew it wasn't that far from the truth. But she disliked the way Harold seemed to take great delight in the thought that she might have scared herself.

"Come to buy some more then?" he said.

Aveline paused, unsure now if she wanted to share her findings with Harold. But she'd never been very good at keeping secrets and he appeared a little more chatty today, which was something, at least.

"No, but I did discover something weird in that book I bought."

"That's funny. My uncle seemed to be freaking out about it, too. What's so weird about it then?"

Joining Harold at the counter, Aveline pulled the book out of her backpack and passed it across.

"Have a look at the final chapter."

Harold turned to where Aveline had indicated, before letting out a loud guffaw.

"Ha! Can't have been much of a story."

Biting her lip, Aveline reached for the book. This conversation obviously wasn't going anywhere. Seeming to sense her irritation, Harold flattened his palm on the page and gave her an odd look.

"Hold on, I mean, yeah, why *would* someone do that?"

"Well, I didn't do it, if that's what you're thinking."

Before Harold had a chance to reply, the bell tinkled and Mr Lieberman swept into the shop. He'd wound a long scarf around his neck and, as he saw Aveline, he began to unravel it like a cowboy twirling a lasso.

"Changed your mind about that book on conveyor belts, eh?" he said, with a wink, though Aveline noticed his gaze flicker to her book that lay on the counter.

"No, it's just that—"

Before Aveline could finish, Mr Lieberman held up a hand.

"Forgive me interrupting, Aveline, but before you go any further, allow me to apologize for not letting you know the provenance of the book I sold you the other day. I think it only fair that I tell you something of the previous owner's history, for I'm afraid it's a rather grim story. It's also fair to say that if you want to return the book once you know more, then please be assured I will happily give you a full refund and—"

Aveline interrupted. "If you're talking about Primrose Penberthy, it's okay, I know all about her."

Mr Lieberman's eyes widened. "You do? How?"

"Her name is written in the front of my book."

"Really, can I see?"

Mr Lieberman came to join Aveline and Harold at

the counter. The old man slipped on his reading glasses and opened the front cover.

"I realized she must have owned the book before me," Aveline explained breathlessly. "So I searched for her name on my aunt's computer and saw the report in the newspaper about her going missing."

"Yes, it's true, I'm afraid. The book came into the shop a few months after she disappeared. Such unfortunate circumstances."

"There's something else, too. Have a look at the final story, *The Lady in the Waves*."

"It's been scrubbed out!" Harold exclaimed, which annoyed Aveline a little. She wanted Mr Lieberman to see for himself.

Running a bony finger down the contents page, Mr Lieberman turned to the relevant page and let out a gasp that lay somewhere between surprise and dismay.

"How bizarre, to say the least. I'm ashamed I didn't notice that before – I would never have put it on the shelf had I known. Who would do such a thing?"

"That's what I've been thinking," Aveline said. "I don't know if it was Primrose…it might have been somebody else."

"Please let me offer you a full refund."

Aveline shook her head. "No, it's fine, honestly. I want to keep it. I'm going to find out more about that story – that's why I came down again. I thought you might know something about it?"

While they'd been speaking, Harold had pulled out a magnifying glass and was busily waving it back and forth over the book, flicking every now and then between the back pages and the front. Aveline watched him suspiciously out of the corner of her eye, unsure what he was up to.

"I think the girl who went missing did it," he said finally.

"Primrose? How can you be so sure?" Aveline pressed, leaning in beside him so she could see what he was looking at. "Surely anyone with a pen can draw black lines?"

"It's easy if you know what you're looking for," he said smugly. "I read a lot of books in here, and once I found one about forgeries and spy stuff. You wouldn't believe some of the cool stuff in there." Harold paused, before glancing back over his shoulder, as if checking that he wasn't being observed.

"What did you find?"

Tossing his fringe, Harold lowered his voice. "It showed how you can match people to the pen they use because of the way they hold it. Just like a fingerprint. Here, have a look through this."

Taking the magnifying glass, Aveline peered at the page. It looked totally different under the lens and she could discern details she hadn't been able to before. But she still failed to see what Harold was getting at.

"I can see where the pen has been pushed hard into the page, but it still doesn't tell me how you know Primrose did it."

Harold's index finger inched into view. Through the lens, Aveline could see where he'd bitten his fingernail almost into extinction.

"Right beside the black lines, you should be able to see tiny ink blots," Harold said.

Waving the magnifying glass back and forth, Aveline eventually saw what he meant: tiny black scratches, like minuscule spiders, where the ink had splattered outwards as the nib had been pressed down.

"I can see them, but what does that prove?"

"Now look where Primrose wrote her name."

Aveline did as directed. Under the magnifying glass, Primrose's signature appeared even shakier. It didn't take long for Aveline to put two and two together.

"It's the same pen, isn't it?" Aveline said, feeling a

satisfied glow, like when she knew the right answer to a quiz question. "Held at the same angle, too. Those ink splatters are identical."

"Correct. Well done, Sherlock," Harold said.

Although he was undoubtedly irritating, Aveline couldn't help but be impressed by his detective work.

"So we know for certain that Primrose was the one who scribbled the story out!" Turning to Mr Lieberman, Aveline asked, "Did you meet Primrose? I mean, how did the book come to be in your shop?"

Mr Lieberman narrowed his eyes. "No, I never did meet her personally. Your book was in a box that somebody left on the doorstep. Happens all the time. People are very kind."

"A box?" Aveline cried. "So there were other books? Did you sell any of them?"

Mr Lieberman reached for his ledger and impatiently swiped through the pages.

"Yes, here we are. It appears the only book that made it to the shelves is the one that's now in your possession."

A quick exchange of glances was all it took.

"Then...shouldn't we have a look at the others?" Harold said. "There might be other scribbled-out stories."

"Or maybe she wrote something in one of her other

books?" Aveline suggested. "At the very least we'll be able to see what else she was reading. That might tell us more about her."

"If I've still got them, which I'm pretty sure I have, they'll be in the back," Mr Lieberman said, being a man who rarely threw anything away. "Come on!"

Plunging into the chaos of the rear room, Aveline and Harold helped the old man pull out box after box, until Aveline sneezed as the dust of years gone by flew into the already musty air. With a soft groan, and a loud click that made Aveline wince, the old man lowered himself onto his knees and reached back between two shelves, where there lurked yet another pile of boxes that had seen better days. Discarding each one in turn, he came to the last one and heaved it out, Aveline craning her neck to see.

"Here we go, I think this is it," Mr Lieberman said.

Removing the lid, they pulled out the box's contents, handling them gently and reverently, like archaeologists removing ancient artefacts from the soil.

"I seem to remember I left these books here because they weren't in very good condition," Mr Lieberman said. "I thought I'd find a place for them one day, but obviously I never got around to it."

The books *were* in poor shape. Some had missing covers. Others had damaged bindings and the pages were falling out. But the titles of the books could still be seen. There was a copy of *Oliver Twist* together with a thin volume of *The Wind in the Willows*, but all the others – and there were six or seven – were about ghosts and the supernatural. There were even one or two that Aveline already owned. Once again, Aveline found herself thinking that she and the girl with the surly frown were a little alike, almost as if she were the perfect person to have found Primrose's book. And with each new discovery, Aveline felt like she was getting to know Primrose better, which was both pleasant and slightly unnerving, knowing what she did now.

Unfortunately, at first glance it appeared that none of Primrose's other books were going to offer up any further clues. She'd written her name in every one, and while they checked to see if the signature looked the same under the magnifying glass (it did), and there were underlined passages and the occasional notation in the margins, no more stories had been deleted and there was nothing from which they could glean any other information about Primrose except that she'd been fond of a scary story.

Soon, they'd removed and examined all the books except one.

But when Aveline pulled it out, the hairs on the backs of her arms started to tingle, like they did sometimes during a storm.

Because the final *book* wasn't a book at all.

It was a diary.

"Everywhere I go it feels like somebody's walking behind me, but they're always hovering just out of sight."
P.P.

Chapter 5

The Lost Diary

"I'm sure this wasn't meant to be included," Mr Lieberman said, running a bony hand thoughtfully over the diary's cover. "I think whoever dropped her books off may not have realized. What do you think we should do, Aveline?"

Aveline took her glasses off and gave them a quick polish. She appreciated Mr Lieberman asking her advice. Most adults simply *told you* what was going to happen next. Being consulted on something as important as this made her like the old man even more. Not that she had any answers.

"I don't know. I mean, I wouldn't want *anyone* reading my diary, but maybe we should see if there's anything actually written in it first? Lots of people buy diaries but forget to ever write in them."

To answer her question, Mr Lieberman opened the diary and held it up for her to see.

This one *had* been used. Quite a lot, too, judging by the number of pages that were filled with small, jumbled writing.

Aveline fell silent as she considered the rights and wrongs of reading further.

"I'm not sure I'd care much if I was, you know, not going to be using it again. And if it means we might be able to discover more about her and maybe even why she went missing, then that's got to be okay, hasn't it?"

Mr Lieberman held up his hands in a gesture of exasperation. "Ach, books I know, diaries I don't."

"I think it's creepy," Harold said. "It's like those people who stare into the coffin at funerals."

Aveline ignored him.

"I mean, we could just have a quick look," she insisted, unable to bear the thought of not seeing what Primrose had written.

Mr Lieberman paused, before handing the diary to Aveline.

"I think I'd feel more comfortable if you made the

final decision. You must be near enough the same age as Primrose, so you're much better placed to understand whatever she's written. And if it's important we can pass it over to the proper authorities."

The old man's argument made sense. Any guilt Aveline had harboured melted away in the excitement of the discovery. If the roles were reversed, and it was she who'd gone missing, Aveline would be more than happy for Primrose to read *her* diary. Besides, all she really wanted to know was why Primrose had felt the need to erase the story in the book. If she came across anything in the diary she felt she shouldn't be reading, then she would simply turn the page and move on.

"Okay, I'll do it."

"Rather you than me," Harold said.

"Nobody's asking you," Aveline snapped.

"Alright, keep your hair on, I was just saying."

Not wanting to read the diary with Harold around, adding stupid comments, Aveline made to leave. It felt like something she should do somewhere quiet and private. Somewhere she could concentrate.

"Let us know if you find anything," Mr Lieberman said as he escorted her to the door, before adding in a whisper, "Don't let Harold get under your skin. He's just bored and, I suspect, more than a little bit lonely."

"I won't," Aveline promised. "See you later."

Mr Lieberman's parting words made Aveline feel a bit guilty about leaving Harold behind. She decided that if she did find anything, she would tell him at the earliest opportunity. But for now, at least, she wanted it to be just the two of them – Primrose and herself.

Not knowing the town very well, Aveline was unsure where would be a good place to settle down and begin reading. In the end she decided on a bench halfway along the beach road. She guessed the seafront would normally be busy with walkers, but the wind carried a chill that nipped with sharp teeth, driving all but the hardiest indoors. It meant that Aveline could enjoy some privacy. Empty chip wrappers blew past like greasy ghosts, but she huddled into her warm clothing and made herself small, before pulling the diary from her backpack.

It was plain and simple, with no pictures or stickers on the cover, just a brief statement of ownership:

Primrose's Diary.

Aveline started at the beginning, her heart fluttering a little as she stepped uninvited into someone else's private world. Much like her own diary, the opening page was a cheerful introduction.

Hello, Diary, this is Primrose. You and me are going to be best friends. We're going to share lots of adventures and I'm going to tell you about my day and what I'm thinking and you have to promise not to tell anyone else, okay? Some days I might not want to talk, but don't take it personally. Sometimes I just don't feel like it.

So, I expect you want to know a bit more about me if we're going to be spending a lot of time together. I'm eleven years old (nearly twelve actually) and I live with my mum and dad and little brother Kevin, who's really annoying and you have to never, ever let him read you. If he does, I'll kill him. I mean it. Kevin, if you're reading this then stop right now or I'll hide your comics.

Anyway, I have short black hair, which my mum says is the same colour as a raven's wing. Not sure if that's good or not. I live in Malmouth, by the sea. We moved here a couple of years ago. It's okay. In the summer we go paddling if the sea's warm enough and look for crabs in the rock pools.

Lots of tourists come in the summer but in winter they all go away and the town gets pretty boring, almost like it's been abandoned. My best friend is a girl called Kelly. I like listening to music (mainly Madness and The Specials) and I'm learning to play the keyboards. I also like reading, mainly about ghosts and haunted houses. After I die I'm going to come back as a ghost and scare everyone who was horrible to me.

Aveline giggled. How strange. She'd had *exactly* the same thought. It felt almost like she was having a chat with a best friend, only Primrose was doing all the talking. It eased her conscience a little, and she didn't feel like such a snooper. She'd never heard of *Madness* or *The Specials* but made a note to look them up.

Resisting the temptation to flick forward to the later entries, Aveline checked her watch. Nearly lunchtime. Aunt Lilian had said her private lesson would go on until early afternoon, so she didn't feel in any rush to get back. She'd only be in the way and she could grab something to eat when she returned. Shifting her legs, she got comfortable again.

I also like watching films about ghosts on TV, although Mum and Dad don't really like me doing it and say I'll end up giving myself nightmares.

Aveline rolled her eyes. *Same here*, she thought. Her mum never stopped going on about that.

But I don't think ghosts are out to get us. I think a lot of ghosts are just unhappy about something bad that was done to them - that's why they moan and wail a lot. If I was horribly murdered, I'd be angry, too. And I think you must get to a point where you're so furious that you refuse to go anywhere else, because you've got unfinished business to deal with. And you want to scare people because you're always really mad about everything. I don't know though. Nobody does really.

Resting for a moment, Aveline took off her glasses and pinched the bridge of her nose. As the clouds thickened, the sunlight faded, painting everything a dull grey. A huge gull watched her every move with hungry black eyes, obviously used to the discarded offerings of picnicking tourists. The way it stared made Aveline think it might be sizing *her* up for lunch, and she stuck a leg out to try and make it fly away, but it only hopped away a few paces before resuming its vigil.

The sense of being utterly alone started to get to her. Reading the diary had made her feel like a part of Primrose's life, even if only for a short time. Now she was back to being on her own, as if Primrose had suddenly jumped up and left. It would have been nice to have a friend to talk to, but they were all back in Bristol, and she'd left her phone charging at her aunt's.

Feathers of rain began to brush her cheek. Popping her glasses back on and pulling up her hood, Aveline tucked the diary away and hopped over the wall that separated the beach from the road. Making her way to the water's edge, she selected the flattest pebbles she could find and tried skimming them over the waves. As each wave crested, black swirls of seaweed appeared in the water, before the wave rolled over and exploded into foam.

Aveline found herself unable to tear her attention away. Something about the dark tendrils of seaweed floating in the water reminded her of…

Hair.

Crying out, Aveline staggered back.

Open-mouthed, she stared at the water, her breaths coming in ragged gasps.

For the briefest of moments, short black hair swirled around a pale frowning face, which strained up towards the surface as if desperate for air.

A face she recognized.

Primrose Penberthy.

And then she was gone.

All Aveline could see now were the oncoming waves, the seaweed simply a natural part of the sea. Shivering, Aveline sat down to give herself a moment to recover.

Oh, Aveline, jumping at your own shadow again, are you?

Hearing her mum's voice made her feel better, even if it came from inside her head. A half-smile crept on to her mouth. She didn't really want to admit that her mum was right, but as far back as she could remember she'd done this to herself. The little girl who wouldn't give up her nightlight until only a couple of years ago, imagining monsters under the bed and faces at the window. She'd even done it to her aunt the previous night. If only Spooking Yourself was a subject at school, she'd be top of the class. Still, it came with the territory. Some girls she knew liked ballet. Others liked football. She liked ghosts. It hadn't been something she'd deliberately set out to be interested in, they'd just sort of crept up on her. Besides, all she'd thought about today was Primrose Penberthy, so no wonder she'd begun to see her everywhere she looked.

And yet...a cold, haunted feeling, buried deep down within her, refused to go away.

Dusting herself off, she made her way quickly back onto the beach road. She wanted to be back in the warm and dry before reading any more of the diary. She kept her eyes fixed on the pathway as she passed the last cottage on the row and its creepy resident with the empty stare, before turning onto Aunt Lilian's street.

"Hello, Aunt Lilian? Are you home?"

Charlie wagged his tail and came to greet her, having now accepted her as one of the pack.

"Hey, Charlie," Aveline said, giving the dog a rub with one hand while picking up a note on the kitchen table with the other.

Gone to supermarket. Food in the fridge. Back soon. Lilian.

Odd. Maybe the lesson had already finished? Filling a

large glass with water, Aveline gulped it down, before pulling out some bread and cheese to make a sandwich. Outside, the waves hissed on the shore, but apart from that the house lay quiet. Taking a huge bite of food to keep her growling stomach quiet, Aveline wandered into the living room.

On the wall were pictures of Aunt Lilian's relatives, including one of herself, taken a couple of years ago. Aveline cringed at the little girl in the picture with the oversized glasses that made her look like an owl. Had she really looked like that? How embarrassing. Ideally she'd turn it around, or at least replace it with a more recent one, but she didn't dare touch her aunt's things. Even placing her glass of water on the coffee table made her nervous.

One framed picture on the wall appeared very old. It was a grainy photograph of a house, typical of the type of fishing cottage she'd seen in Malmouth. She stopped chewing for a moment.

Aunt Lilian's.

It wasn't whitewashed and there were fewer plants in the front garden, but there was no mistaking its dimensions, the windows and the door in the exact same positions. She could even see the pear tree, though it wasn't as old and gnarled as it was now.

After finishing her sandwich, cleaning her plate and making sure she returned it to *exactly* where she'd found it, Aveline flopped onto the sofa and retrieved Primrose's diary. Charlie the dog came to join her and laid his head on her legs, which made her feel a bit better about being in this creaky, crooked house on her own.

As the shadows gathered, she found the point where she'd left off and started to read again.

At first the diary continued quite normally. Aveline learned that Primrose liked a boy called Matthew at school, but he could be really annoying at times.

Sounds a bit like Harold, Aveline thought with a grin.

Primrose also argued with her mum about a pair of jeans. Her little brother, Kevin, was being a pain. She'd been to the cinema to watch a film called *Ghostbusters*, which had made her nearly "pee herself" laughing.

Yawning, Aveline rubbed her eyes. But as she finished the page, the last sentence leaped out as if it'd been written in fiery letters.

Bought a new book today about ghosts in Dorset and Cornwall. Looks scary. Going to start reading it tonight. Hope there's something about Malmouth in there!

This was it.

Exactly what Aveline had been searching for. Impatiently, she flicked through the next entry, which chiefly concerned more day-to-day stuff. But the following page made another mention of the book.

Hello, Diary, last night I finished that ghost book I told you about. It was great and I know a lot of the places mentioned in the stories. It makes me want to go and visit them. Not on my own though. The only story I didn't like was the last one. It's set here, in Malmouth, which was super creepy. I've been thinking about it all day. The weirdest thing was that when I was walking home from school I thought I saw someone at my bedroom window looking out at me. Maybe my dad is right and I need to stop reading ghost stories all the time.

After that, the diary became noticeably different: the entries were shorter; mentions of her friends Matthew and Kelly became less frequent, as if they were no longer on Primrose's mind. The book – or rather the final story in it – appeared to have taken a little of the fun out of Primrose's life. There were mentions of how lonely Malmouth felt, which reminded Aveline of what Harold had said about it.

Last night I woke up in the middle of the night because I had this horrible nightmare. In my dream, someone was bending over me and trying to touch my face. It was a lady and she had long dirty hair and I could smell seaweed on her breath. The worst thing was her eyes.

She didn't have any.

All I can remember after that is screaming really loudly and my dad ran in and asked me what had happened, and I couldn't even speak, I was shaking so much. He took me down to the kitchen for a hot chocolate and I told him what I'd dreamed and he said not to worry about it because everybody has bad dreams from time to time and it was probably something to do with being stressed out at school.

I didn't tell him about the story in the book, but I know that's why I had the nightmare. Wish I'd never read it.

Charlie growled softly, a low rumbling in his belly.

"What's got into you?" Aveline said, reaching down to tickle his ears, which seemed to calm him.

What an awful dream. Primrose seemed to be becoming increasingly...*haunted*. Aveline decided there and then to tell Harold about it and see what he thought. A gut feeling told her that Primrose's growing anxiety was linked in some way with her disappearance, but it could just as well be a fanciful theory. A second opinion could be useful.

Aveline leaned back and took off her glasses. The room had become gloomy as the afternoon had stretched on and she'd been squinting to read Primrose's spidery writing. Without her glasses, the room blurred out of focus and Aveline squeezed her eyes shut.

When she opened them again, a silhouette blocked the doorway.

Aveline sat up quickly, blinking furiously and disturbing Charlie, who leaped down.

Shadows obscured Aunt Lilian's eyes. "Sorry if I startled you, Aveline."

"Oh, Aunt, you made me jump."

"Where has your friend gone?" Aunt Lilian said, untying the scarf from around her neck.

Aveline frowned. "It's just us two," she said, pointing to Charlie, who wagged his tail in agreement.

Flicking on the overhead lights, Aunt Lilian peered suspiciously around the room, her face visibly paling. "Oh, I must have been mistaken. I thought for a minute that—"

Aveline had never seen her aunt lose her composure before. She waited for her to finish the sentence.

"Never mind," Aunt Lilian said, folding and unfolding her scarf. "Do you want something to eat?"

Not waiting for an answer, she walked through to the kitchen.

Watching her go, a niggling feeling that all was not well crept along Aveline's forearms. Giving them a rub, she tucked Primrose's diary away and headed upstairs for a shower.

At the sink, Aunt Lilian washed some potatoes under the tap, staring out at the darkening afternoon with a frown.

"Do you ever feel like something bad
is about to happen? I've been getting that
a lot lately."
P.P.

Chapter 6

Footsteps

All that evening Aunt Lilian appeared distracted. Twice Aveline saw her visibly twitch – once when a log burst and spat in the fire, and again when Aveline accidentally banged her tea mug down too hard on the table. Normally her aunt sat as still and as rigid as a statue.

But it wasn't just Aunt Lilian that seemed jumpy. The whole house felt unnaturally tense, like a simmering pan coming slowly to the boil. Usually Charlie dozed peacefully in front of the fire, but tonight even he seemed restless, too. Every now and then he would whine softly, unable to settle into his regular routine. If she'd been at home, Aveline would have put some music on, but she didn't dare suggest that here. Something told her that

Aunt Lilian wouldn't share her taste in music.

As the evening wore on, the tension became almost unbearable. Her aunt began knitting, the *clack-clack-clack* of the needles like a ticking clock. Aveline stared at her phone, picked up her book, put it down, played with her hair. She couldn't relax. The diary and its unnerving contents played on her mind. She found herself glancing occasionally into the corners of the room, convinced that she'd seen something move. She knew she would read the diary to the end. She'd come too far to stop. Only she wanted to wait until her aunt had gone to bed. This felt like a private affair between herself and Primrose. Part of her wished she'd never picked it up. Or the book of ghost stories. They appeared to be leading her to a place she wasn't wholly sure she wanted to go.

Just as Aveline felt a yawn coming on, they heard a series of thumps make their way across the ceiling. A thin drizzle of dust drifted slowly down to the floor from the overhead light.

In her short time here, Aveline had heard the house make some pretty odd noises – popping and banging and wheezing as the temperature changed and pipes warmed and cooled. She'd seen that the house was old, but even so.

This sound was unmistakeable.

Footsteps.

"Did you hear that?" Aveline whispered.

Aunt Lilian paused before answering, as if considering how to respond. "Yes. As I said to you before, the house is old and somewhat eccentric."

Something in her tone suggested fear, despite her rational explanation. And there was no doubt in Aveline's mind that the noise *had* been footsteps. In truth, nobody could have entered the house without them seeing or hearing anything. That left only one explanation, as far as she could see.

The house was haunted.

That would certainly explain the weird happenings she'd experienced. But she didn't have the courage to suggest anything of the sort to her aunt, who'd already made her feelings known on the subject of the supernatural. Yet, with the handprint on the window and now this, the longer Aveline stayed, the more she became convinced that it wasn't just the two of them living here.

Aveline excused herself and her aunt decided to go to bed, too. Normally Aunt Lilian would stay up late, but tonight Aveline felt relieved that she'd have someone to go upstairs with. The lights didn't quite reach to the top of the staircase.

Aunt Lilian clicked off the lamps and placed the guard in front of the fire. Reluctantly, Charlie left his warm spot in front of the fireplace and trotted into the kitchen, before curling up in his basket. When her aunt locked the back door, Aveline noticed she tugged on the door handle three or four times to check that it was secure.

"Aunt Lilian, I saw that picture on the wall earlier, the old one of the house – where did you get it?"

"Oh, I don't know. I think I found it in the attic. Lots of junk up there. Anyway, come on, let's get to bed."

At the top of the stairs, both of them paused.

"Well, goodnight then," Aunt Lilian said. "Don't forget, I'm just across the landing if you need me."

It seemed an odd thing to say, almost as if Aunt Lilian could sense Aveline's growing nervousness about the house and its *quirks*. But it did have the effect of making Aveline feel a little less uneasy. After hearing her aunt's bedroom door close, Aveline grabbed the diary and jumped into bed. This was it. The moment she'd been both dreading and excited about. Pulling the sheets up to her chin, Aveline ran her hand over the cover of the book, the sense of anticipation almost unbearable. Did Primrose have any inkling of what was about to happen to her? And was there more to her disappearance than simply sleepwalking? Swallowing hard, Aveline opened the diary. There were only a few pages left and the entries were still short. It felt like time was running out, as if Primrose were struggling against something unseen.

Hello, Diary, I hope you're feeling better than I am. I'm having trouble sleeping at night. No more nightmares, thankfully, but I can't stop thinking about that lady from my dream. She was just someone in an old story at first, but I can't help thinking that by reading about her, I've somehow made her real. I'm afraid to go to sleep. I've got bags under my eyes and keep yawning at school. My teacher even noticed and asked if I was okay. I've got a confession to make, too. Promise you won't tell anyone? I scribbled out that story in the book that's been creeping me out so much. I hope it'll make me forget about the creepy lady. I feel bad but it's my book and I don't want anyone else to read that story in case the same thing happens to them and they start seeing people that aren't really there, too.

Finally, Aveline had her answer.

She understood now why Primrose had done it. While frustrated at being denied a chance to read the story for herself, Aveline felt desperately sorry for her friend from the past. Imagine being that afraid of a story…

Aveline realized that this was proof Harold had been right about the pen, too. She needed to let him know that his suspicions had been correct – credit where credit was due. His talents obviously extended beyond setting the world record for Number of Chips Stuffed in a Single Mouth.

Lowering her head, she read on, eager to see what else she could learn.

Dear Diary, I thought there was someone in the house this evening when I got home. Mum and Dad had gone out to pick Kevin up from football. The front door was wide open and the house stank like a fishing boat. I didn't go in and waited in the front garden until they came home. Dad went in and checked, but there was nobody there. He said they might have forgotten to close the door because they were late and in a rush. Doesn't explain the smell though. It reminded me of what the harbour smells like after a storm, when all the driftwood and rubbish gets washed up on the beach. All those horrible scarecrows around town are getting on my nerves too. What's that all about anyway? Dad says it's just some crazy local Halloween thing, but why would you want to put a load of scarecrows up that look like sick kids? Dad asked if we wanted to make one but I told him no way. It's stupid and creepy.

Aveline chewed on her bottom lip, Primrose's fear leaking out of the diary like a trail of black smoke. So the scarecrows happened every year. That was interesting. It was also another thing that she and Primrose agreed on – they were unsettling, to say the least. Aveline hadn't forgotten her two creepy scarecrow neighbours only a few hundred metres away. Burrowing down under the covers as far as she could go, Aveline turned the page.

Dear Diary, someone sat down on my bed in the middle of the night. I woke up but there was nobody there. But I don't think I dreamed it. I felt a real heavy weight and there was that weird smell again. It's hard to describe how I feel, but it's like being chased, only you can't see who's chasing *you. I tried to talk to Kelly about it, but she said I was imagining things. I'm not though. You believe me, don't you?*

By now, Aveline wanted to take the diary back to the bookshop and bury it in the box where they'd found it. At first it had been fascinating. Now it was quickly becoming terrifying, but she couldn't stop. She had to get to the end.

Dear Diary, today I think I saw a ghost. The same woman who I dreamed about. She was standing on the beach as we were walking home from school. She had long black hair and looked dirty, like she hadn't eaten or washed for a long time. Just standing there in the water. I grabbed Kelly and pointed to the beach, but I swear as soon as Kelly looked, the woman wasn't there any longer. I didn't imagine it though. Or maybe I did. I don't know – it feels like I'm going crazy. I'm scared. I've always wanted to see a ghost, but when you actually see one for real it's not like you expect. It's horrible and freaky and the worst thing is that nobody believes you.

A dog barked in the night. Aveline stared nervously at the window. The curtains moved slightly, blown by an invisible breath.

Dear Diary, didn't go to school today. Stayed in bed. I don't want to go outside in case I see that lady again, but I don't want to stay home either. It's Halloween tomorrow and some of my friends have asked me if I'm going out but I can't face it. I donn't know what to do. Maybe if I just try and stop thinking about her she'll go away, but I'm not sure that'll do the trick. Because I think I've worked out who the lady is and, if I'm right, she's been coming to Malmouth for a very long time now and isn't about to stop. The worst thing is, I think I know what she wants too.

She wants me.

It was the final entry.

Frantically, Aveline flicked through the rest of the diary, but the remaining pages were blank. She reread the last entries. So Primrose belicved she was being haunted by a lady she'd read about in the ghost book. It seemed too crazy to be true, but what other explanation was there for the things she'd experienced?

The really uncanny thing was, tomorrow would be the anniversary of Primrose's disappearance.

Halloween.

Aveline had read Primrose's final diary entry on the same day of the year that it had been written. Also, if Primrose had believed – rightly or wrongly – that someone or something was after her, then it seemed more than just a coincidence that she went missing shortly after.

Poor Primrose.

She'd tried to do everything she could to help not only herself, but others, too, by scribbling out that story.

If only she hadn't deleted the one clue that might help solve the mystery of her disappearance.

The next morning, as Aveline debated what to do about the diary's unsettling revelations, she heard a knock on the front door. Aunt Lilian was upstairs in the bathroom, so reluctantly she went to answer it.

Harold was huddled on the doorstep, rubbing his hands. The tip of his nose and cheeks glowed a frosty pink. Surprise registered on his face as he glanced up and saw Aveline frowning at him.

"What are you doing here?" he said.

"I'm staying here, what's your excuse?" Aveline replied.

"With Ms Jones? Oh. I didn't know. I'm...um...here for a lesson."

Aveline couldn't help but laugh. "You have private lessons with my aunt?"

For once Harold seemed stuck for a smart answer. The rest of his face reddened and he nodded. As soon as she saw him blush, Aveline regretted laughing. Hurriedly, she replaced her smile with a more serious expression.

"I mean, my aunt is an excellent teacher, I know she only takes on really smart pupils."

This seemed to do the trick and Harold shrugged his shoulders, as if silently conceding that, yes, he was indeed *very* smart.

"Did you find anything in that creepy diary then?" Harold said as she led him into the kitchen and called her aunt down. Aveline held a finger to her lips and motioned in Aunt Lilian's direction. For the moment she wanted to keep it a secret, just in case it proved to be unrelated to Primrose's disappearance.

"Yes, I did actually," Aveline whispered. "Primrose admitted crossing out that story in my book."

"Ha! Told you, didn't I?" Harold said loudly.

"Shush!" Aveline said, as Harold didn't seem to grasp what a finger held against the lips meant. "That's not all either. You wouldn't believe some of the things she wrote in there. She thought that—"

"Hello, Harold, you're early for once," Aunt Lilian said, entering the kitchen. "You should have warned me, I could have died from shock."

"Hello, Ms Jones," Harold mumbled, glancing nervously at Aveline as if checking that she wasn't laughing. She wasn't. In fact she felt relieved that it wasn't just her who seemed a little anxious in her aunt's presence.

As Aunt Lilian led him into the living room, he turned back to Aveline and hissed loudly, "I want to know what you found. Wait for me, I won't be long. You'll need my help again."

Once he'd gone Aveline rolled her eyes, but knew it would be useful to discuss her discoveries with him – after all, he'd been helpful once already.

It turned out to be almost an hour before he appeared again. Aveline told her aunt she was going with Harold to get some fresh air, then they walked slowly along the seafront, which gave Aveline the opportunity to update him on what she'd found.

"Do you think we should tell the police?" she said.

The wind whipped Harold's fringe, making his long hair swirl in every direction like he'd been trapped in a tumble dryer. Cursing, he angrily swept it aside.

"What, tell them that the girl who disappeared thought she saw a ghost? Yeah, great idea, I'm sure they'll be *really* interested in investigating that."

The maddening thing about Harold, Aveline decided, was that he would often make a good point, only to spoil it by saying it in a really sarcastic tone of voice. About to snap back at him, she followed the advice that her mum had given her once and took a deep breath before replying. It seemed to do the trick.

"We don't need to mention *that* part," Aveline said, as calmly as she could. "But we do need to let them know about the diary. There might be stuff in there that helps the investigation. Do you know where the police station is?"

"Yeah, but you can do the talking. I don't want them thinking I believe in all this ghost stuff, too."

As they reached the end of the beach road, Aveline gasped and pointed. "Look!"

A large porcelain doll had been hung outside one of the houses on a length of rope. It pirouetted slowly and sinisterly around in the breeze, its glassy eyes and crafty smile making it appear as if it knew a secret about them. Aveline couldn't stand to look at it for long. It hung there like a whispered threat.

"Ugh, what is it with the people in this town?" she exclaimed. "There are two scarecrows down where my aunt lives and now this. Hasn't anybody told you lot that you're supposed to put out pumpkins and plastic skeletons on Halloween?"

"I didn't make the rules," Harold said, throwing up his arms in a show of innocence. "But I suppose it is a bit creepy to an outsider."

"But you do go out trick-or-treating?"

"No. The streets are even more deserted on Halloween. I told you this town was dead."

Aveline's mouth dropped open. "What, even the little kids don't get dressed up? Do you know *why* everyone's so weird about it here?"

"No idea. They all dress up as lobsters on the first of May and push each other around in wheelbarrows, too, and I don't know why they do that either."

Aveline laughed, sneaking a sideways glance at Harold, though all she could see was hair. "Primrose thought it was really creepy, too, you know."

"What's that?"

"Oh, just something Primrose wrote in her diary. She said the scarecrows looked like a bunch of sick kids."

Harold snorted. "I'd say she was right about that. Now you know why all the tourists leave at the end of summer."

It only took a couple of minutes to reach the police station, a small building set back from the high street with a solitary patrol car parked outside. Inside, there was a waiting room and a counter with a glass window, alongside an invitation to ring the bell for assistance. While Harold skulked behind her, looking uncomfortable, Aveline banged the palm of her hand down on it a few times, like she'd seen people do in films.

"Yes, can I help you?"

The woman behind the counter wore normal clothes and a stern expression that suggested she didn't appreciate being summoned by a fidgety girl with messy hair and big glasses. Sensing she needed to be quick, Aveline placed the diary on the counter and got straight down to it.

"Hello, we've found this diary. It belonged to a girl called Primrose Penberthy. She went missing. I thought you might want to look at it."

A brief look of surprise flickered across the woman's face. Obviously she'd been expecting them to report a cat stuck up a tree or a stolen bicycle. You couldn't treat a missing person case lightly.

"Could you tell me the name of the missing girl again please?" the woman said.

"Primrose Penberthy," Aveline replied. "P-E-N—"

"It's okay, I know how to spell it, it's a common enough name around these parts," the woman said, a little curtly. "And do you know when Primrose was first reported missing?"

"The thirty-first of October," Aveline confirmed.

"Last year?"

"No, the thirty-first of October 1984."

The woman laid her pen down and frowned at Aveline. "1984?"

"Yes."

"Oh. I see."

Aveline could sense the woman's relief. In a matter of moments, this had gone from a potentially urgent situation to a couple of amateur detectives investigating a case that was over thirty years old.

Panic over.

"And what is it in the diary that makes you think the police need to look at it?"

"Someone was after her," Aveline blurted out. "I mean,

she *thought* someone was after her, and I think it's connected to a story in a book I'm reading, but I can't be sure because it's crossed out."

"And who did she think was *after* her?" the woman pressed.

"I don't know exactly, but I think it might have been a ghost."

Behind her, Harold coughed loudly.

"Um…or maybe she'd just imagined it," Aveline added. "But it sounded very much like a ghost to me, because I've read a lot about them."

She turned and glared at Harold, who swiped his finger across his throat while hurriedly shaking his head in a *no-no-no-don't-say-anything-more-about-ghosts* gesture. But the cat was out of the bag. Aveline hadn't intended to mention anything supernatural and cursed inwardly. The disdain on the woman's face was plain to see and Harold wouldn't be able to resist saying *I told you so*.

"Well, thank you both for bringing this…matter to our attention," the woman said. "I'll pass your information on to the duty sergeant and they'll contact you if they have any further questions."

"Should I leave the diary with you?" Aveline asked.

"No, but if you could leave me a contact phone number

where we can get hold of you, along with your name and address…"

A few minutes later, Aveline and Harold walked despondently out of the station. Aveline knew she'd made a hash of things, but thought their discovery would have generated a *little* more excitement. The police didn't even want to see the diary. Perhaps sensing her frustration, Harold had wisely decided not to crow about it.

They paused to stare at some fudge in one of the many ice-cream shops that did a roaring trade in the tourist season before switching to a rather sad and lonely existence. It wasn't really ice-cream weather. The *Closed* sign on the door told them business wasn't exactly booming.

"I think it's safe to say we won't hear from them again," Aveline said.

"Nope, reckon you're right."

"But I do think Primrose saw a ghost. She didn't think anyone would ever read her diary, so why bother making stuff up?"

"Maybe," Harold said, chewing on a nail. "But lots of people think they see ghosts. Doesn't mean they're real."

"I think it was real to her. That's all that matters. Same as when you're young and you think there are monsters under the bed. They're not real either, but it doesn't stop you being terrified. I mean, if she thought a ghost was after her, she could have been running away from it and fallen into the sea. That's possible, isn't it?"

Harold pursed his lips. "Who knows?"

"Well if we can find out what that last story was about in my book, then maybe *we'll* know?"

Not waiting to see if Harold followed her, Aveline headed towards the one place where they might find answers.

Somehow, she needed to discover more about the story of *The Lady in the Waves*.

And going back to the bookshop seemed as good a place as any to begin.

"It's so cold. I can hardly hold my
pen straight. When does summer start again?"
P.P.

Chapter 7

The Vanishing Girl

The tattered old sign on the bookshop door said *CLOSED*.

"My uncle must have popped out," Harold said. "He's always doing that."

Aveline grabbed hold of the doorknob and gave it an angry tug.

"It's locked," Harold said unhelpfully, before adding with a sly smirk, "but I do know a way we can get in."

"From that spy book you told me about?" Aveline said. "I know that people can open locks using hairgrips – is that what you're going to do?"

Harold's mouth rose into a wide grin. "Yes, I have a top-secret device for this type of challenge," he said, slowly reaching into his back pocket. "It's called…a key!"

And with that he inserted it into the lock and gave it a quick twist.

"There you go," he said, pushing the door open. "Much easier than fiddling around with a hairgrip, don't you think?"

Aveline pushed him inside. "Ha, ha, very funny." His jokes were awful but she couldn't help grinning.

"Remind me again, what are we looking for?" Harold said, closing the door behind them. "My uncle already said there are no other copies of that book."

"I don't know exactly," Aveline said, glancing around. "Maybe the story appears in other ghost books?"

"Worth a look, I suppose," Harold said. "Let's try in the back."

"Hang on a second, what's this?"

Aveline's attention had been drawn to a noticeboard just inside the door. Pinned to it were a series of flyers for local businesses and attractions. A mole-catcher offered *No Mole, No Fee*, alongside a phone number. There was an advertisement inviting people to enter Malmouth's Country Show, although it was two years out of date. You could enrol in pottery classes. Learn guitar. Have your dog walked by a professional dog-walker called Barbara.

Windows could be cleaned for *the lowest price in the south-west*. And tucked just behind a notice that asked people to look out for a missing cat called Jake, there was a very strange flyer. Aveline bent forward for a closer look.

An Evening of Magic, Myth & Legend

A presentation on local folklore, hosted by
Mrs Edith Fitzwilliam.
Sunday 17th September, 7.15 p.m.
Malmouth Public Library,
The Parade,
Malmouth.
Refreshments will be served.

Aveline reached out and carefully removed it from the wall.

"I think I may have found the answer," she said, thrusting the flyer out for Harold to see.

"Not sure about that, this lecture happened over a month ago," he said. "Besides, what's a talk on magic got to do with anything?"

"Well, the lady who gave this lecture *must* know about local folklore," Aveline said. "Maybe she's heard of the story in the book? All we have to do is find out where she lives and go ask her."

"What if she lives in London?"

Aveline sighed. "She might live in Timbuktu, but we won't know unless we ask, will we?"

A knock on the window made Aveline turn. Outside, Mr Lieberman grinned at them through the grimy panes. A second later, he walked in.

"Good to see you two are busy keeping the bookshop running in my absence." He beamed. "I had a very important appointment with a large scone and a pot of jam. You can't beat these cream teas, you know, a most marvellous invention."

Before he could get into his stride, Aveline held up the flyer for him to see. "Mr Lieberman, do you know who this lady is?"

Taking out his reading glasses, Mr Lieberman popped them on his nose. "Ah, yes, Edith Fitzwilliam. A most learned and respected authority in these parts. She brought some books in once and we had a long chat about local customs." A second later his eyes widened. "Of course, you think she may know something about our missing story! Ach, why didn't I think of her sooner?"

"We thought it was a worth a try," Aveline said, feeling a surge of hope. "Do you know where she lives?"

"Yes, of course, I made a note of her address and phone number. I always do when someone brings me books."

Reaching down behind the counter, he pulled out a ledger and blew a cloud of dust off the cover. He leafed through the pages, then turned it around and held it up for Aveline to see.

Mrs Edith Fitzwilliam.

"There she is," he said, jabbing his bony finger at the entry. "An old lady, yes, but full of life. Made me feel ancient. I'll call and see if she's free."

Mr Lieberman's excitement sparkled in the gloomy bookshop. Aveline felt excited, too, but at the same time her stomach rumbled like an angry dog and concentrating on anything other than cheese sandwiches was hard.

She'd been so keen to get out of the house she'd forgotten to eat lunch.

"Okay," she said. "I'd better be getting back though or Aunt Lilian will be thinking I've disappeared, too."

Harold promised to let her know if they managed to arrange a meeting. After saying her farewells, Aveline pulled her coat tightly around her as she left the shop. The street felt like a wind tunnel, and she picked up her pace, eager to get back to a warm house and a big plate of food. She should have been happy. They appeared to have made a breakthrough. Yet she didn't feel as satisfied as she should. If anything, she felt more nervous than ever. Something stirred in Malmouth. What exactly, she had no idea, but beneath her thick coat, her skin felt cold and clammy.

Patches of blue sky glowed between black clouds. Water ran along the gutters, but the rain had stopped for now. As always, Aveline's eyes were drawn towards the sea, which this afternoon was a turbulent blend of turquoise and slate. For a moment she paused to take in the drama, filling her lungs with the tangy, briny air that swept her mind clean like a stiff brush. Behind her, the two kid scarecrows outside the fishing cottages watched in silence. Aveline could feel their dead, dull gaze boring into her shoulder blades and so she quickly moved on.

Halloween seemed much more fun back in Bristol. But things were different here. The monsters were real.

As she let herself in through the front door, she called out, "Hi, it's only me."

She expected Charlie to come and greet her, but his basket lay empty. No note had been placed on the kitchen table either. But as she stepped into the living room, Aveline saw that actually there *was* somebody here.

Facing the fireplace stood a small figure. A girl, by the looks of it. She wore an olive-green parka, jeans and red Dr. Martens boots. Aveline had always wanted a pair herself and gave them an envious look. This must be a pupil of her aunt's, Aveline concluded, left to wait while Aunt Lilian busied about getting herself ready upstairs.

"Hello, are you waiting for my aunt?"

The figure turned her head slightly, as if she'd only then become aware of Aveline's presence. The hood of the parka was zipped up so far that nothing of her face could be seen, except just a glint of light in one black eye.

"I'm waiting for the lady," the girl said, her voice surprisingly deep.

Aveline smiled at that. Her aunt would love being referred to as "the lady", though it sounded very formal to her ears.

"She's probably upstairs," Aveline said, trying to peer into the hood without making it obvious. "But she should be down any minute, especially if she knows you're here."

The girl didn't respond, but that was okay. Aveline knew what being shy felt like.

"I like your boots," she said, in an effort to break the ice.

The girl sat down on the sofa, hunching forward and wrapping her arms around her legs as if she was cold. "My mum bought them for me," she said.

"I asked my mum for some but she said we couldn't afford them."

"You can have mine if you like," the girl said. "I don't really use them any more." Which struck Aveline as odd, seeing as she had them on. Curiosity started to get the better of her. A lot of girls her own age often seemed to have endless confidence and would launch into long conversations without any hesitation. Aveline liked this girl's...stillness. She didn't seem in a rush to impress anyone.

"Do you live here?"

"I used to," the girl replied. "Do you?"

"No, I'm just staying with my aunt for a few days. It's a bit strange though, isn't it? Sometimes it feels like I'm the only person in town."

"I know what you mean. It's the sea, I think. It's just so huge and empty, it makes you seem alone even when you're not."

"Glad I'm not the only one. Are you cold? I can ask my aunt to light the fire if you like."

"I'm always cold."

"Fancy a hot chocolate then? That's what my aunt gives me when I need warming up."

The girl turned her head in Aveline's direction. Just for the briefest of moments, the living-room lamp illuminated a pale face with a large forehead and a choppy hairline. The eyes crinkled a little, as if deep down in the folds of her parka, the girl smiled. For a second Aveline had an odd sensation that the two of them had met somewhere, but before she could think where that might be, she noticed a pool of water had gathered at the girl's feet.

"Oh no, you're soaked through! Did you get caught in the rain earlier?"

The girl shook her head. "No. I got caught by… someone. And now she's coming for you."

A cold blast of wind slammed into Aveline's back and the front door banged hard as it was pushed open. The girl's eyes widened and she glanced over Aveline's shoulder.

"Brrr, it's so cold out there I thought my nose was going to drop off!" Whirling around, Aveline saw Aunt Lilian march in with Charlie's lead in one hand. "Come on, Charlie, don't be dawdling on the doorstep, unless you want to help pay my heating bill. Aveline, you're back, I see, I gave up waiting for you. Did you get lost?"

"Um, yes. I mean no," Aveline said.

Startled by her aunt's arrival, she turned back towards the fireplace.

The girl had gone.

She glanced at the floor.

Bone dry.

Aveline's mouth dropped open as she let out a soft gasp. She couldn't quite believe what she was seeing. Or rather, what she *wasn't* seeing. Hastily she gave her glasses a quick polish, as if blaming them for this inexplicable situation. It would have been impossible for the girl to leave without being seen or heard. So what exactly had happened? Aveline could smell something in the air, too. Slowly fading now, but it was an aroma she'd become quite used to.

Salt water.

Aveline began to shake uncontrollably. Now she knew why the girl had seemed so familiar. It was *her*. She'd seen her photograph in the newspaper. Those dark eyes that glinted so fiercely. That unmistakeable choppy hair that looked like it had been cut with a blunt knife. Aveline realized something else, too – when she'd asked the girl where she lived, she'd said she used to live *here*. Thinking about the way she'd said it made Aveline realize that she hadn't meant Malmouth at all.

"Are you quite alright, Aveline? You look awfully pale," Aunt Lilian said, hanging up her coat.

"Do you know who lived here before you?" Aveline said in a trembling voice.

"Before me? An old couple, I believe their name was Farnham. Mrs Farnham sold the house after her husband passed."

"What about before that?"

"I've no idea," her aunt said abruptly. "Might I ask why you're suddenly interested in the history of this house? I'm sure it's all very humdrum. Oh my, look, your poor little hands are shaking!"

Aunt Lilian rushed across and took Aveline's hands in hers before proceeding to give them a vigorous rub. Aveline's mum used to do the same to her when she was little.

"So is there anything the matter, Aveline, or have you just decided to be pale and interesting today?"

Aunt Lilian was trying to make her smile, but it took all of Aveline's willpower not to let herself collapse on to the floor. Leading her to the sofa, Aunt Lilian struck a match and held it against the kindling in the fireplace until it caught. Soon the room filled with the sound of crackling wood. A thin band of greyish-blue smoke drifted through the room.

Like a ghost.

Aveline wondered whether to tell her aunt what she'd seen. But she feared that Aunt Lilian would think she was making stuff up, trying to get attention. Or worse, that she was simply being ridiculous. She didn't want to be thought of as a stupid child.

"Oh, I just scared myself."

Aunt Lilian's eyes narrowed. "Are you absolutely sure? Because you know you can tell me if you're upset, or unhappy, or somebody's said something to you that they shouldn't have."

"No, I'm fine. Like I say, I just gave myself a fright."

"Would a cheese toastie improve matters, do you think?"

"Maybe," Aveline said, forcing a smile. In truth, her appetite had all but died.

As her aunt busied herself with slicing cheese and toasting bread, Aveline sat on the sofa, watching the flames flicker and twist. If Harold were here right now, she'd tell him everything. He'd give her his honest opinion on the matter, even if it was one she didn't want to hear. Yet without her mum here, she had to put her trust in her aunt. She took a deep breath – even if her aunt thought she was being ridiculous, she had to say something about what had just happened or she'd burst.

"Aunt Lilian," she called. "You know that book I bought from Mr Lieberman, the second-hand one?"

"Yes. What about it?"

"I think it belonged to a girl who used to live in this house. She went missing. Today is actually the anniversary of when it happened."

"Really? How do you know this exactly?"

Aunt Lilian's voice carried a note of warning, but Aveline couldn't stop. Not now she'd started. If she didn't tell someone soon, she might start to think she'd dreamed the whole thing.

"I found a news report on the internet about her. And…I think I saw her, too. In the house. Just now."

For a few moments Aunt Lilian hummed under her breath, slicing the cheese toastie in half and putting it on a plate. Emerging from the kitchen, she placed it on the coffee table.

"So that's why you look scared half-to-death, is it? What did you see?"

Aveline took a bite of her toastie and forced herself to swallow.

"I saw a girl standing in front of the fireplace. She was dripping wet. I thought she must be one of your pupils. We spoke for a while and she told me that someone's coming for me."

"Oh. I see."

The silence felt thick and oppressive. Aunt Lilian examined the palms of her hands, before raising her head with a searching look that made Aveline want to groan. She knew what that look meant.

"I'm not saying you're mistaken, Aveline. But you're in a strange house, in an unfamiliar town, and you're probably missing your mum, and you've been reading about ghosts, and it's all very windy and wild here, I know. Plus you're hungry and tired. And, well, all these things may have combined to make your imagination play tricks on you."

Now Aveline knew what Primrose had meant in her diary, when she'd said that the worst thing about seeing a ghost was that nobody believed you.

"But what about the footsteps that we heard the other night?"

"Hot water flowing into cold pipes."

"And when you thought somebody was in the house but it was just me and the dog?"

"Shadows on the walls. Tricks of the light."

"But surely you don't think I imagined having a conversation with a girl who wasn't there?"

At this, her aunt shuffled in beside Aveline on the sofa and gently took her hand. The fire spat out an ember, which cooled against the hearth, its light slowly dying. Aveline sensed that they'd come to a crossroads in their conversation. She wasn't sure what direction they were going in next, only that her aunt appeared to be building up to something. Eventually, Aunt Lilian spoke, her voice low and even, as though not wanting to disturb the stillness.

"You know, Aveline, I haven't been truly honest with you and for that I apologize. You are indeed correct: a girl who used to live in this house did go missing and her name was Primrose Penberthy. I found out myself shortly after I bought the place. You see, when I discovered that old picture of the house, I became curious and decided to do a little research of my own. I thought it would be interesting to find out more about the history of the place. That's when I learned about Primrose. But, to be honest,

I thought no more about it. A tragic event for all concerned. But *all* houses have histories and many of them are very sad. That's just life. In truth, I soon forgot all about it. That was, until I saw her name in the book you bought."

Aveline felt relieved to have been proven right. But also a little angry.

"So why didn't you mention it when I bought the book?"

"For the very reason we're now having this conversation. I didn't want to scare you. I know you like reading about ghosts and you're a highly imaginative and creative girl, so I could easily guess your reaction if I told you that the house you were staying in was once the home of a girl who disappeared. I thought you'd be seeing ghosts around every corner. And I suppose, in one sense, I've been proven right."

"But you believe me, don't you – that I saw her?"

Aunt Lilian squeezed her hand. "I hate to admit it, but yes, I do. One thing I know with utter certainty is that you're not a liar or a mischief-maker. I'm just saying that there *could be* an explanation other than ghosts. Our brains are very complicated pieces of machinery and can do incredible things, especially when we're upset or worried. That's all I meant."

Aveline wondered if her aunt said this for her own benefit. Knowing your house was haunted would surely make for some very uncomfortable evenings, and in a few days Aunt Lilian would have to be here on her own. But still, she couldn't let the matter rest. Not after what Primrose had told her.

"Okay, but even so, she said – Primrose, I mean – that someone – *she* – was coming for me. You don't think I'm in danger, do you?"

Aveline could tell that her aunt was working through the issue in her mind, the cogs slowly clicking round and round.

"Well, it's no wonder you're terrified. What an upsetting thing to be told. But listen and believe me when I say that you will *never* be in danger as long as I'm here, Aveline. If there is indeed a threat of a supernatural nature, then we'll deal with it together."

Before she could continue, a single, heavy knock on the door made them both jump.

"Who's that?" Aveline whispered.

Hesitantly, Aunt Lilian got up to answer the door, while Aveline crept along behind her, doing her best to stay hidden.

Knock. Knock. Knock.

The coats on the back of the door trembled slightly.

Keeping a safe distance, Aunt Lilian unlatched the door and swung it open.

A tall, rangy silhouette filled the doorway. A voice creaked like an old floorboard.

"Ach, good afternoon, Lilian! I trust I'm not disturbing you on this most inclement afternoon?"

"Mr Lieberman!" Aveline cried.

"And there's the very person I wanted to see," Mr Lieberman said. "Come, Aveline, we have an appointment to keep!"

"Why can't we just have a normal
Halloween like everybody else?"
P.P.

Chapter 8

Night of the Scarecrows

Harold loomed out from behind Mr Lieberman like the old man's shadow. With his scraggy hair and lean dimensions, he reminded Aveline of the scarecrows in the nearby gardens. He had the tip of his middle finger inserted in his mouth, which he gnawed at like a dog chewing a bone.

Aunt Lilian invited the two of them in from the cold and showed them into the living room, where they nervously stood with their hands in their pockets. As Aveline returned to her seat, the old man's eyes narrowed.

"Are you alright, my dear? You look like a vampire has paid you a visit."

"She's fine," Aunt Lilian snapped. "So what's all this about, Ernst?"

Mr Lieberman shot Aveline a nervous glance.

Stepping in, Aveline explained to her aunt, as quickly as she could, about how they'd *all* become embroiled in the mystery of Primrose's disappearance. She didn't tell Mr Lieberman and Harold what her aunt had just told her, or that she'd seen – and spoken with – Primrose only a short while ago. That could wait until later. By the time she'd finished, her cheeks were red from the heat of the fire and she sat back to catch her breath.

"One person who may be able to shed some light on the subject has called to say she's free this afternoon," Mr Lieberman finished. "Edith Fitzwilliam, do you know her?" he asked Aunt Lilian.

"I don't believe so," Aunt Lilian said.

"She's an expert on local folklore," Mr Lieberman told her. "Aveline and Harold here thought she may be able to help them. Why don't you come with us?"

"Yes, come on, Auntie, you're part of this now," Aveline pressed, their conversation still fresh in her mind. For once, she wanted her aunt close by.

Aunt Lilian looked at them each in turn, before grimacing.

"Very well, lead on, Ernst," she said. "I haven't experienced so much *excitement* in a very long time."

Mr Lieberman clapped his hands and together they wrapped up in all their layers and headed out into the darkening afternoon.

"She lives on the outskirts of Malmouth," Mr Lieberman said as he unlocked his car and gestured for them to climb in. "But it's not a long drive, just a few minutes up the hill."

Aveline was relieved they didn't have to walk. As the car turned onto the beach road, a fierce wind blew in from the sea and hit it squarely on its side, rocking it on its suspension. Beyond the shore, white tops rolled towards them like a herd of horses in a race to be first. Harold sat beside her in the back seat. He had a book pushed between his legs, which he fiddled with as Mr Lieberman drove. Aveline watched him out of the corner of her eye. He seemed restless and agitated, as if working up the nerve to say something. In the end, her patience ran out.

"What's that book about?" she said.

"This one?" he said, trying and failing to act nonchalant. There was only one book on the backseat of the car.

"Yes."

"I found it in the shop today after you left and I… um…put it aside for you."

"Really?"

"Yeah, well, nobody's ever going to buy it," Harold added quickly, handing it to her. "It's about all that weird stuff you're into."

"Oh…thanks," Aveline said, wondering whether to feel complimented or insulted. Taking a quick look, she saw that it was about the history of Halloween. Very fitting, considering the date. Normally the type of book she'd love to read. But before she had a chance to examine it further, she found her attention drawn in the opposite direction.

"Oh no, there are even more of them," she cried, pressing her nose up against the window and staring open-mouthed at the fishing cottages. Almost every home now had a scarecrow of some variety in their garden. Although they were all different shapes and sizes, each one was clearly intended to represent a child. With their oddly shaped heads, grubby clothes and crooked limbs, they resembled a class from the School of Nightmares.

"Happens every year," Mr Lieberman said. "A most perplexing tradition. Of course, living in a small flat above the bookshop, I don't really have the space to adhere to the custom myself, but your parents put something out, don't they, Harold?"

"Yeah, it's a small boy made from fibreglass with a slot in his head. Used to be a charity box that people would put coins in. Dad got it from a vintage shop a few years ago. Looks like Pinocchio's poorly brother."

"But what does it all mean?" Aveline pressed. "I haven't ever seen anything like it."

"I believe it has something to do with the notion that on Halloween, spirits roam the night," Mr Lieberman said, crunching down a gear. "I think they may even be intended to represent said spirits, but I can't be wholly sure. We can ask Mrs Fitzwilliam, she's bound to know more."

Aveline shivered under the scarecrows' eerie stares. It was like being watched by an audience of the undead.

And it only got worse.

As Mr Lieberman's old Mini groaned up the steep road that led out of Malmouth, Aveline was dismayed to see that the houses up here were also observing this strange custom. Those homes that didn't have gardens had hung long-limbed mannequins in their windows. Some had big cheesy cartoon smiles, which lent them a horribly malevolent air. Some were made from straw, others from bits of wood. There were more repurposed shop-dummies, too, like the first one she'd seen. These were undoubtedly the most unsettling as at a glance they might pass for real children, were it not for their lifeless eyes.

Within minutes they pulled up outside a small cottage.

Through the window, an old, lined face peered out at them. It was framed by long snow-white hair, which had been tied into bunches and fell down over the woman's shoulders. Aveline's first impression was of someone who spent a lot of time outdoors. They clambered out of the car and walked up a path that led to the ivy-covered porch. The door swung open and Mrs Fitzwilliam stepped out, scowling up at the clouds as if daring them to unleash any rain.

"Come in, come in, it's far too cold to be standing outside on a day like this," she said, her voice crackling like an autumn bonfire.

Aveline smiled, dipping her head slightly before pushing back her glasses. The old woman stooped like a hilltop tree bent by years of gales. Cocooned in a thick woollen shawl, she leaned heavily on a knotted walking stick. Aveline studied Mrs Fitzwilliam, wondering how old she actually was. Despite her age, she radiated the warmth of a summer day. Aveline could easily imagine her pottering around this crumbling cottage with trays of home-baked biscuits and pots of nettle tea. And she decided that she wanted to live in a snug little cottage like this one day, too, surrounded by paintings and rugs and comfortable couches that slumped in the middle.

"You, too, Mr Lieberman, enter, enter. You're almost as old as me, far too old to be out wandering in this weather. Oh, I see you've brought young Harold with you as well. Look how tall he is, and so much hair!"

As Harold hid his embarrassment, Mr Lieberman bowed and held out his hand.

"Allow me to introduce Aveline and her Aunt Lilian," Mr Lieberman said.

Taking Aveline by the arms, Mrs Fitzwilliam looked her squarely in the eye. "You are *most* welcome." Turning her attention to Aunt Lilian, they shook hands. "You, too, my dear, it's nice to have guests."

"Thank you," Aunt Lilian said. "What a charming cottage."

As the adults exchanged small talk about the horrible weather, Aveline found herself distracted by a large hand-drawn map of Malmouth. Trying to find her aunt's cottage, she noticed that alongside the harbour wall, the mapmaker had written:

The Lady's Lookout.

While *Lady* was a common enough word, she recalled the title of the crossed-out story.

The Lady in the Waves.

Not to mention that Primrose had said she was *waiting for the lady.* It seemed an uncanny coincidence.

Mrs Fitzwilliam ushered them all into the front room, where a fire crackled in the grate, filling the room with a wonderful thick warmth. Someone had spent a lifetime making this house feel welcome and Aveline already felt it was going to be hard to leave once the time came for them to return home.

The furniture was old but comfy, made of dark wood and covered with tartan blankets and plump cushions. Bunches of herbs were tied to the walls with twine, presumably to dry out. A large bookshelf dominated one end of the room, and Aveline found herself drawn to a series of pictures on the wall. One showed a circle of dancing foxes. Another showed a stag standing on a misty moor, its antlers like polished branches. Yet another showed a set of stone ruins under moonlight. It all felt very atmospheric, and with the smell of woodsmoke and rosemary filling the air, the house had a magical feel to it.

"Sit down, my dears, sit down and I'll fetch us some tea," Mrs Fitzwilliam said.

Aveline nibbled her knuckles. Harold twisted a strand of hair round his finger. Mr Lieberman held his knobbly hands out towards the fire. Aunt Lilian plumped the cushion behind her, arranging it into a nice, neat square. Despite the welcoming atmosphere, Aveline couldn't quite relax, and sensed that the others were a little nervous, too. All being well, they were about to find out some important information about the missing story in the book, and that could prove to be a vital clue in the mystery of Primrose's disappearance. And yet she wasn't wholly sure if she wanted to know. It was like waiting for the results of an exam at school – desperate to discover how you got on, but also wanting to cover your eyes and stick your fingers in your ears in case it turned out to be bad.

Mrs Fitzwilliam shuffled in with a tray. Mr Lieberman got up to help her.

"Here we go, my dears, some tea and cake – go on, help yourselves, I've no one else to eat it for me."

Aveline's stomach rumbled and she helped herself to a thick slice, which was dark, treacly and utterly delicious.

"So you're Lilian's niece?" Mrs Fitzwilliam said.

"Uh-huh," Aveline nodded, unable to offer a more detailed reply due to the amount of cake in her mouth.

Turning to Aunt Lilian, Mrs Fitzwilliam held out a teapot. "I'm sure you must be very happy that Aveline's chosen to spend some time with you."

"I'm not sure *chosen* is the right word," Aunt Lilian said drily. "But yes, I'm delighted she's here."

"We have need of your local knowledge, Edith," Mr Lieberman said, for once eager to cut to the chase. "If I were a more learned man then I would have left you in peace, but we have a question to which there is no answer to be found in any of my available resources, and as an antiquarian of the local area, Aveline thought that you may be able to help solve our conundrum."

"I'm glad you all came," Mrs Fitzwilliam said. "What can I help you with?" Her crinkled face turned to Aveline.

Aveline glanced at Mr Lieberman for reassurance. The

old man nodded back, his twinkling eyes shouting encouragement. Reaching for her backpack, Aveline pulled out the book of ghost stories and passed it to Mrs Fitzwilliam.

"I bought this from Mr Lieberman – that's how we met."

"What's this now?" the old lady said, turning the book in her fingers. "Ah, local ghosts, I'm not sure I've read this particular edition."

"But you're familiar with the stories?" Mr Lieberman said, edging forward on his seat.

"I don't know, let me see," Mrs Fitzwilliam said, before opening the front cover to squint at the title page. "Oh yes, *Blackmarsh Cove*, used to be quite a lawless place back in the day. Best not to go there at night, by all accounts. And yes, *The Phantom Coach*, a friend of mine claimed to have seen it but none of us believed her. She was always one for a tall tale. These stories are all familiar to those of us who've lived around these parts for a long time. Everywhere has its ghosts, don't they, Mr Lieberman?"

"Ach, indeed they do," Mr Lieberman conceded. "But there's one tale in particular we'd like your help with, isn't there, Aveline?"

Aveline came and kneeled beside Mrs Fitzwilliam's armchair.

"Look at the last story in the book," she said. *"The Lady in the Waves."*

A log shifted in the fire. Mrs Fitzwilliam showed no emotion as she inspected the lines of black ink that concealed whatever words were once there. Removing her glasses, she sighed.

"I think I know this story. Do you know why it's crossed out?"

"The previous owner of this book did it. Her name's Primrose Penberthy. You can see it written at the front. She disappeared. I think her disappearance might be connected with this story, but we can't say for certain until we know what it's about."

"I remember Primrose," Mrs Fitzwilliam said quietly.

"You met her?" Aveline cried. "What was she like?"

"Only once or twice, but she came across as a quiet and intense girl. Just my sort of person. But why do you think her disappearance is linked to this story?"

Returning to her seat, Aveline took a deep breath. "I've read Primrose's diary. Mr Lieberman and I found it in his shop. She didn't like that story and after she'd read it she started to write some really weird things."

Mrs Fitzwilliam angled her head and raised her eyebrows. "Such as what?"

Aveline tried to remember the exact words. "She said that she'd seen a face at her window, and then she had a nightmare that someone came into her bedroom, and the final entry mentioned something about knowing what she wants: *She wants me*. It felt like the lady she'd read about in the book had come to life. Do you know what *The Lady in the Waves* is about?"

Mrs Fitzwilliam laid her teaspoon on the saucer with a soft clink.

"Yes, I do. I can understand why Primrose didn't like it, it's a very dark tale."

Aveline felt Harold shift his weight in her direction.

Mr Lieberman's eyes flashed, like a streak of lightning across a storm cloud. "Are we on the right track then?" he said. "Could Primrose's disappearance somehow be connected with the final story?"

"How about I tell you all the story and you decide," Mrs Fitzwilliam said. "Why don't you put another log on the fire, Mr Lieberman?"

Flames leaped onto the dry wood as he did so. Mr Lieberman helped himself to more tea. Aunt Lilian took a tiny nibble of cake, apparently more out of politeness than appetite. Mrs Fitzwilliam's eyes grew misty, as if she'd suddenly left all of them behind and wandered off. Then she blinked and looked at them each in turn, as if reminding herself of where she was and what she was doing.

Then she began.

"I'm not sure I want to read any more ghost stories. Maybe Dad was right."

P.P.

Chapter 9

The Lady in the Waves

The fire crackled and hissed. Aveline watched Mrs Fitzwilliam closely, noticing that one of the old lady's hands trembled ever so slightly.

"Well, now, supposedly this all happened a long time ago," Mrs Fitzwilliam said. "I can't be sure of the exact dates and the facts tend to become confused as these tales get told again and again. But there's no doubting it's based on a real event. As you know, there's no smoke without fire, is there, Mr Lieberman?"

The old man stuck out his lower lip and nodded gravely, though he made sure not to interrupt her flow.

"If I've got the right story, then *The Lady in the Waves* is about Cora Poole. She lived here in Malmouth but was something of an outcast on account of the fact that she moved here from London. Folks said that she thought herself a cut above everyone else and looked down her nose at them. But I can tell you that, in truth, folk around here aren't the most welcoming. It's said that if you aren't born within earshot of the sea, you'll always be an outsider. So there you have the truth of the matter: she was probably nothing more than lonely and didn't feel very welcome here, so kept herself to herself.

"Because of this, she devoted all her time to her children. She'd married a local fisherman and they'd had two daughters. Apart from her husband, they were her only friends. Cora schooled them at home and, by all accounts, she absolutely doted on them, giving them everything they could ever want despite not having two pennies to rub together. They were never apart, this mother and her daughters, and the girls stuck to her like limpets to a rock. Small and dark they were, exactly like their mother, so in time the locals started calling them the three witches, after the opening scene in Shakespeare's *Macbeth*. Every day, at sunset, Cora and her two girls would walk along to the end of the harbour wall to watch for her husband's fishing boat coming home. It got to the point where they became familiar figures, almost like a landmark that the fisher folk would look for, to guide them into port.

"Now this went on for many years, until the day of the storm. If any of you have ever lived in a fishing community for a long spell, you'll know that storms are the one thing that people here fear above all else. City folk stay indoors in front of the fire and watch the rain running down the windows and think no more of it. But if you're far out at sea, a storm can be a death sentence, and there's many a memorial around the coastlines of this country to testify to that."

Aveline pulled the cushion out from behind her and placed it across her knees, hugging it for comfort. Outside, the wind howled. Flecks of rain scarred the windows of the cottage. Aveline imagined Cora Poole, standing on the sea wall, her dress flapping in the wind as she clutched her daughters tight.

"This storm was a big one," Mrs Fitzwilliam continued in a low, even voice. "The sort that comes along only once every decade. The sort where you could sail out on the most perfect day you've ever seen – the sea could be as still as a millpond and the sky could be as blue as the cornflowers in my back garden – but within a few minutes everything changes. The breeze picks up. The waves swell. You might see black clouds on the horizon that appear to be miles away, but they swoop down on you so fast that you don't even have time to weigh anchor. This is what happened back then and they didn't have weather forecasts or radar or satellites to warn them. They were hit by a storm like they'd never seen, the sort that can pull the roof off your house and blow down hundred-year-old trees like matchsticks.

"Of course, when the winds started to pick up, the first thing anybody thought of were the folk out at sea and they all rushed down to the harbour. Nothing brings a fishing community together like a storm. There are no lords or ladies when a storm breaks. Arguments and disputes are put to one side. Everyone's in it together, with one purpose in mind – making sure the boats get home safe. So there they all were, crowded onto the shoreline, watching the horizon and squinting between the swells, hoping and praying for a glimpse of sail. And miraculously, one by one, the boats appeared, being tossed around like ninepins of course, but there nonetheless. Of course they still had to get themselves back into the safety of the port, but the high cliffs of the bay here act as a natural shelter, and once they got within sight of the shoreline, they had a fighting chance. Thanks to the skill and experience of the captains, the boats limped into the bay, and everyone breathed a sigh of relief. The fishermen were hugged by their families, and taken off for a pint of beer at the pub and a hot bath."

"But what about Cora's husband?" Aveline burst in. "Did he come back safely, too?"

Mrs Fitzwilliam's expression darkened. The fire shifted uneasily in the grate, sending a spiral of sparks up the chimney.

"That was the problem, you see, Aveline. In all the panic, everybody forgot about Cora Poole. And her husband was the only one who had yet to return. There she stood, out on the sea wall, her daughters beside her, leaning into the wind, one hand shielding her face from the rain as she peered out at the crashing waves, hoping against hope for the sight of a white sail. It was far too dangerous to be up there, and when the townsfolk finally noticed, they shouted at her to come back in. But as you can imagine, what with the crashing surf and the screaming wind, she couldn't hear them. People said there was a dreadful feeling of inevitability about it. Everybody seemed to know what would happen next, but they were too fearful to help, for to walk out on that wall invited death.

"They saw it coming in from far offshore. The seventh wave in the cycle. A sheer wall of water rising out of the sea like some terrible dark god. Once again, they called and waved their hands, but Cora remained too fixated on the horizon to notice the danger. The wave met the harbour wall like a steam train. The ground shook. It crashed over the wall and swept Cora and her daughters into the sea. A moment later it was as if they'd never been there. The townsfolk ran to the shoreline with ropes and lanterns, but of course it was hopeless. The sea had claimed them for its own."

Aveline had been biting her bottom lip throughout the story. Mr Lieberman appeared similarly engrossed, tiny pinpricks of light gleaming in his eyes. Harold was busily removing what little was left of his fingernails. Aunt Lilian gripped her cup and saucer tightly. Outside the sky darkened, the gloomy prelude to another long autumn night. Tonight was Halloween, the same day Primrose had disappeared.

But the story wasn't finished yet.

More logs were thrown on the fire, and Mrs Fitzwilliam switched on a couple of lamps, which had the effect of keeping the gloom at bay, for a while at least.

"So what happened after that?" Aveline said in a whisper. "Did they ever find the bodies?"

"Sometimes the sea never gives back what it takes. But more often than not, the drowned will wash up on the shore. This time neither of those things happened. As is so often the case with these coastal storms, the next day turned out lovely, all blue skies and sunshine. Despite the previous night's horror, the boats went out as normal. Even such a terrible tragedy didn't stop the business of fishing. But then, not far out, a boat snagged something heavy in one of their nets. Sensing something untoward, the crew hauled it in. Terror spread across the faces of the fisher folk, and they hurriedly crossed themselves. In the net, Cora Poole hung lifelessly, her limbs all askew. One of the crew said she appeared to be dancing. But the most unsettling thing, the thing that they never forgot until their dying day, was that where Cora's eyes were supposed to be, there were only dark, empty holes. The crew of the fishing boat made their way back as if the Devil himself was on their tail, and while there are no records of what happened to poor Cora, presumably they buried her in the local churchyard – though as far as I know, none of the headstones has her name on it."

"What about her daughters?" Harold said. "Did they ever find their bodies?"

"And what happened to her husband?" Aveline added.

"Sadly, while her husband did indeed return safely, the daughters were never found," Mrs Fitzwilliam replied. "Only Cora, who returned from the depths to stare accusingly at the men and women who'd forgotten her."

"But that's not the end either, is it?" Aveline asked.

Mrs Fitzwilliam buried her hands in the folds of her cardigan and shivered. "No. That wasn't the end of the matter, Aveline, otherwise I don't suppose she'd be making an appearance in a book of ghost stories! Now this is the part where fiction probably takes over from facts, so you mustn't let it scare you."

Aveline squeezed the cushion, unable to conceal her impatience. "It's okay, I don't scare easily," she said, knowing that this statement wasn't strictly true. Aunt Lilian raised her eyebrows but said nothing. Aveline was afraid that to admit her fear might make Mrs Fitzwilliam unwilling to reveal the end of the story. To come this far and not know how the story finished would be unbearable.

"Well, as time went on the incident wasn't forgotten, but memories of that terrible day did begin to fade a little. That was until a year or so later, when a local man claimed to have seen Cora Poole walking on the harbour wall. Everyone treated his account with a mixture of respect and suspicion. People here are a superstitious lot, as you can tell by the number of ghost stories connected with the area. Perhaps there were also a few guilty consciences. But the man in question was also known to be fond of a drop or two, a regular in the local pubs. So an element of doubt crept in. People assumed he'd had one too many and had simply imagined it, or had mistaken one of the townsfolk for her. Cora Poole wasn't the only person in town who walked on the harbour wall.

"But the next night, one of the local children disappeared. A girl, I believe. Anyway, search parties were dispatched to all the usual places where mischievous children are normally found. As the night wore on, the parents became increasingly concerned, but there was no sight of the missing child. It was as one of the search parties returned home that they saw her: Cora Poole, standing on the shoreline, those terrible empty eyes staring out to sea. And holding her hand was the missing girl. But as the search party ran towards her, Cora walked off into the surf, dragging the child down with her. The poor mite was never seen again.

"And that's how the legend of *The Lady in the Waves* started. They say that once a year, on All Hallows' Eve, Cora comes ashore, searching for a child to replace the ones she lost."

Aveline thumped the sofa. "The scarecrows! *That's* what they're for!" she gasped.

"What?" Harold said, screwing his face up in confusion. "They actually have a purpose?"

"It makes total sense once you know the story," Aveline explained. "They're exactly what they're supposed to be: pretend children."

Mrs Fitzwilliam smiled.

"That's right, Aveline. Clever you. That's how it all began, you see. Folk would leave these scarecrows outside to confuse Cora. Because she couldn't see any more, she couldn't tell what was real or not. So as long as you put the decoy out, your children would be safe. After that it became part of local life, though I wonder how many people in this town actually remember the legend behind it."

For a while the only sounds were the moans of the wind and the *tap-tap-tap* of rain on the windows. Mrs Fitzwilliam poured some more tea. Mr Lieberman stuck a poker into the fire and made a big show of moving the logs around.

"Primrose," Aveline said softly. "That's what happened. Cora Poole took her. Her family didn't make a scarecrow like they should have done. She said as much in her diary."

"I'm not sure that's true, dear," Aunt Lilian said.

"But do you think it *could* be true, Mrs Fitzwilliam?" Aveline asked. "Primrose read the story. She said she'd seen a strange lady, and afterwards her home smelled of the sea. It all makes sense."

Mrs Fitzwilliam exchanged an uneasy glance with Mr Lieberman and Aunt Lilian.

"I don't know, Aveline. I suspect not. It's far more likely to have been a terrible accident that just happened to coincide with Primrose scaring herself with a story. But perhaps it's best if you were all going before it gets dark. The weather isn't getting any better and I'm sure Mr Lieberman doesn't want to be driving home at night."

An unsettled feeling rose in the room like a sea mist. Mr Lieberman jangled his car keys as he got to his feet.

"That seems a perfectly sensible suggestion. Thank you for your time, Mrs Fitzwilliam, and for explaining the story to us. I know I'll be locking my doors tonight!" Mr Lieberman said with a wink.

Aveline knew Mr Lieberman was doing his usual trick of trying to lighten the mood, and although it didn't reach the cold feeling in the very marrow of her bones, she appreciated the effort.

They all got up and said their goodbyes to Mrs Fitzwilliam.

"Thank you for the tea," Aunt Lilian said. "Perhaps you'd like to come down to my cottage sometime and let me return the favour."

"That would be very nice indeed, thank you," the old lady said, seeing them to the door.

As Aveline passed by, Mrs Fitzwilliam touched her lightly on the arm.

"You know, my dear, perhaps these old customs have some truth to them," she said softly, giving Aveline a very pointed look. "*You* know what I mean, don't you?"

Aveline hesitated, before nodding. She'd had the same idea herself.

As they drove back down the winding hill road into town, Aveline stared at all the different effigies outside the houses, imagining Cora Poole stumbling between them, reaching out to run her cold, desperate hands over the faces.

While Aunt Lilian and Mr Lieberman discussed the poor state of Malmouth's roads, Harold whispered across to Aveline.

"You know, I did see something interesting in that book – the one I gave you earlier."

"Really? I thought it was just me who's into that stuff."

"Well, I suppose we're into it together now," Harold said. In the dark of the car, Aveline couldn't tell if he was blushing or not. "But yeah, so I read a few pages before we came to get you. Give it here a sec and I'll show you."

One of the pages had been bookmarked. Harold pointed to it. It had an old black-and-white drawing of a skeleton with a scythe, but the type underneath was too small for Aveline to read in the gloom.

"What does it say?"

"It says that in the old days Halloween used to be called Samhain. People believed it was the one day of the year when the dead could actually visit the living. Something about the veil between this world and the next being at its thinnest. I thought it might be connected in some way."

Aveline was about to ask what that had to do with anything, but then she quickly realized that it had *everything* to do with what had happened. It seemed that perhaps Harold was something of a dark horse. Smarter than he let on, certainly.

Because whether he knew it or not, he'd just given her the final piece of the jigsaw.

"Thanks, Harold."

"See you tomorrow maybe. Can't see myself going out tonight."

"No."

Mr Lieberman pulled to a halt outside Aunt Lilian's cottage.

"Thank you for the lift, Ernst," Aunt Lilian said. "It would be nice if you were able to come for tea, too, sometime?"

Aunt Lilian appeared to have softened towards the old bookseller. Aveline had a sudden image of her aunt and Mr Lieberman walking arm-in-arm along the seafront. What an odd couple they'd make.

"Ach! I would like nothing better. It would do me good to escape the dusty confines of my little kingdom for an hour or so. Thank you! Goodnight, Aveline, and don't worry. I'm sure Cora Poole is at rest and has no desire to come and visit any of us. You'll be safe with Lilian."

"Okay, thanks," Aveline said, not feeling wholly reassured.

As they got out of the car, their heads filled with the roar of the waves and they felt the sting of salt water on their skin. Up above, brooding clouds billowed in from the sea like colossal grey ghost ships. A storm brewed, and Aveline knew time was running short.

With the daylight almost gone, she knew what she had to do.

She needed to make something that looked like a child. And fast.

"I only really feel safe when I'm in bed.
Nothing can get me once I'm under the covers.
Not even ghosts."
P.P.

Chapter 10

Somebody's at the Door

Holding a lantern aloft like an explorer entering an Egyptian tomb, Aveline peered up into the attic. A cold draught of air blew against her cheeks. The fusty smell of forgotten things made her nostrils flare in alarm.

Aunt Lilian called up from the bottom of the steps.

"You know, I'm not sure I like this idea, Aveline. Be careful up there, please. I promised your mother I'd give you back in one piece."

"I'm okay, don't worry, I'll be quick," Aveline replied.

Placing the lantern to one side of the attic hatchway, she clambered up the last step and hauled herself through. There was just enough room to stand in, though she had to duck beneath the wooden beams that criss-crossed the roof. Like all attics, it felt creepy, the lantern casting long shadows into the far corners, so that there always appeared to be movement – dark figures scurrying for cover out of the corner of her eye.

"Are you okay?"

"Yes, fine," Aveline called back a little impatiently.

Thick sheets of grey cobwebs hung between the rafters, the work of generations of spiders. *How did they survive?* Aveline thought. She doubted there was a single fly up here.

Boxes of junk lay scattered between the rolls of yellow insulation. Dotted in among them were other abandoned objects, though whether they belonged to Aunt Lilian or previous occupants, Aveline could only guess. What she wanted didn't appear to be up here. She didn't need a dusty rowing machine. Nor did she want to play an ancient version of Scrabble or Monopoly. She had no desire to go rooting through a rusty toolbox or go camping. There were some spare clothes she could use to dress a scarecrow, so she dragged them out into a pile. But she really needed to find something to go below that – something she could use as a head, arms and legs.

"Everything okay?"

"Yes, just looking through the junk."

Kneeling down, she began to rifle through some of the cardboard boxes. There were books in some, which she made a mental note to pass on to Mr Lieberman. No chance of them finding a new home while they were stuck up here. The next box contained kitchen utensils. In another lay a set of cracked cups and saucers. There were piles of old paperwork in others, sheets of paper covered in numbers that made absolutely no sense whatsoever. Most of this stuff needed chucking out.

Then she spied a pair of old wooden skis.

Legs.

Tucking them under her arm, she spied something else. A long-past-its-best beanbag, grey with dust.

A body.

Aveline still hadn't found something to use as a head, but then she had a brainwave. Picking up a cardboard box full of papers, she turned it upside down and emptied them out. It wasn't round, but they might still be able to fashion it into something vaguely human. She'd seen worse fancy-dress costumes.

At that moment, the light coming through the open hatch flickered.

"Aveline, you're not stepping on any wiring up there, are you?"

Aveline checked beneath her feet. "No, I don't think so?"

A second later, a buzzing noise sounded somewhere down below, then the house plunged into darkness.

"Oh damn. The fuses must have blown. They do that sometimes during a storm. Best you come down now, Aveline, I'll need the lantern to fix the fuse box."

Disorientated in the darkness, Aveline stumbled towards the faint grey square of light that marked the entrance to the attic. Lowering the skis, clothes, beanbag and box down, she gingerly backed down the steps. A pair of cold, knobbly hands gripped her ankles.

"Careful now, I've got you."

Aveline allowed herself to be guided down the ladder. In the light of the lantern, Aunt Lilian's thin face appeared like a mountain ridge, all shadows and sharp edges. She glanced at the materials Aveline had gathered together. Disapproving lines appeared on her forehead.

"And that's what you're going to use? Honestly, Aveline, I think we'd be better off just locking the door and going to bed early, but I suppose it won't do any harm. In the meantime, I'll try and get these lights back on."

"Okay, but hurry, please."

Aunt Lilian drew Aveline into her arms and squeezed

her tight. For once her embrace didn't feel quite so thorny.

"Don't worry, you'll be fine. We'll both be fine. There's nothing in the night that isn't also there during the day."

Aveline wasn't sure about that. What Harold had told her made total sense of something she hadn't been able to get her head around until now. Ghosts didn't come and take people.

Unless...the old superstitions about Halloween were true.

In which case, then tonight was the one night when the spirit of Cora Poole could return. That would also explain why she'd seen Primrose earlier. And from what Aveline had learned today, it would be foolish to ignore her warning. Not that she had any intention of doing so.

A thunderous shower began, hammering on the roof so hard that Aveline couldn't hear her own footsteps. Each time it seemed the wind couldn't blow any harder, it reached a new crescendo of fury, like a whistling kettle left to boil itself dry. Aveline thought back to earlier and the storm Mrs Fitzwilliam had described. Hopefully the roof had been bolted on securely and wouldn't be ripped off, too.

"I think there's a trip switch down here," Aunt Lilian

shouted up the stairs. "Shouldn't be long now."

"Okay."

Aveline felt her way along the landing to the bedroom. The window let in just enough light so she could see. Kneeling on the floor of her room, Aveline pushed her glasses up and scowled. She'd never built a scarecrow before and didn't have the faintest idea where to start. Hastily, she tugged a pair of leggings over the skis and held them up. They looked sort of like legs; extremely skinny ones that bent at one end.

But they would have to do.

Next, she attempted to push the tops of the skis through the worn material of the beanbag. Grunting with the effort, she finally broke through the fabric, only to find herself covered in a pile of polystyrene balls.

Thumping the floor in frustration, Aveline stood up and kicked the beanbag, sending another burst of white entrails onto the floor.

The room lit up.

At first Aveline thought that Aunt Lilian had got the lights working, then she realized it was actually a flash of lightning. She started to count: one…two…

The immediate crash of thunder told her that the storm had arrived over Malmouth. Crossing to the window, she wiped at the pane, which crackled as the rain hurled itself against the glass.

Outside, the sea resembled a pan of boiling water. Spouts of foam exploded upwards as the waves crashed against the beach and the harbour wall. Even in the relative safety of the bay, the fishing boats lurched from side to side as if shaken by invisible hands. Yet Aveline's attention lingered on the dramatic scenes for only a moment before she saw something that made her step back from the window in alarm.

On the harbour wall, a solitary lamp did its best to hold back the darkness. Underneath it, she could just make out a ladder, which led down into the water, presumably so people could climb down to the beach when the tide went out.

As she watched, a pair of bone-thin arms broke through the surface of the water, reaching up to grasp the glistening iron rungs.

Aveline held her breath.

Then, like some terrible insect, a twisted figure scuttled up the ladder before hauling itself onto the stone walkway. Strands of long ragged black hair were lifted up by the wind, swirling around the person's head like a swarm of angry flies.

Something about the way the figure stood seemed horribly unnatural. Hunched shoulders. Bent neck. White arms stretched out as though frozen stiff. Long fingers clenching and unclenching, as if their hands were still numb from being in the cold sea. Aveline willed the figure to move again, so she might be able to glimpse something human about them.

Something *normal*.

But deep down, she knew who it was.

And she knew they'd run out of time.

Suddenly, the figure broke into a stride along the harbour wall, and even through the fury and murk of the storm, Aveline glimpsed skin that was too pale to belong to someone living. For the first time in her life she understood the phrase *blood-chilling*, for it felt as if freezing salt water ran through her veins.

"She's here," Aveline whispered.

Her first reaction was to grab her aunt and run. But where would they go – to the next house along? If this truly was a night when the locals feared a nocturnal visit, they might think twice about answering a knock on the door. And what if they ran into Cora Poole on the way? Something told Aveline that out there in the raging storm, they'd be defenceless.

Primrose.

The answer came unbidden into her mind. Primrose had been taken, but had come back to send Aveline a warning. That meant she cared about her, didn't it? If anyone knew what to do, Primrose might. But what if she *couldn't* come back again? Did the dead only get one chance on Halloween? Maybe Primrose had already used her opportunity to warn Aveline? There might be a more detailed explanation in the book Harold had given her. But Cora Poole had risen from the waters. Aveline didn't have time to decipher the rules of All Hallows' Eve.

Turning to the bed, Aveline snatched up the diary.

"Primrose, if you can hear me, please come and talk to me again."

But no matter how hard she focused on willing Primrose to appear, she remained alone in her bedroom, with only the sound of the screeching winds for company.

"Aunt Lilian?" Aveline called.

She crept out onto the landing and made her way to the top of the stairs.

"Auntie, are you down there?"

A muffled voice called back.

"It's no good, I can't find these damn fuses. I think they're in the cellar, I won't be a minute."

"But I saw her, Aunt – Cora Poole!"

The only reply she heard was the distant thump of footsteps as her aunt continued her search for the elusive fuse box. Deciding to go and find her, Aveline crept down the stairs. But as she neared the bottom, a misshapen shadow flitted across the front door.

A second later the handle rattled gently.

Charlie barked once, then whined pitifully.

The handle started rattling again, louder this time, becoming a blur as somebody furiously wrenched it up and down.

Praying that the lock would hold, Aveline glanced around. To get down to Aunt Lilian in the cellar she'd have to go past the front door and through the kitchen. Not only did she want to avoid going anywhere near the front door, hiding in a dark cellar didn't seem like the wisest move. She needed to get to safety, only there appeared to be nowhere safe to go.

As Aveline hesitated, the door handle stopped rattling.

Charlie whined once more, then fell silent.

A moment later, there was a soft click, followed by a slow creak as the door swung open. A chill wind rushed into the house. Dried leaves scuttled over the flagstones like crabs.

Aveline couldn't cry for help. Her tongue felt swollen, her throat constricted. Her heart beat far too quickly in her chest.

Then she heard a voice. Quiet as a whisper, yet it struck Aveline like a shouted command.

"This way."

Over by the fireplace, Primrose beckoned to Aveline. The hood of the girl's parka was still drawn up, hiding everything but two eyes that caught the reflection of the flames in the twilight of the living room.

"Come on, quickly."

Aveline hesitated for only a second, her instinct telling her that Cora Poole wanted her and not her aunt. Aunt Lilian would be safer if she left.

As a crooked shadow spread out across the kitchen floor like an oil slick, Primrose took off, leading the way. Sprinting through the living room and out through the back door, Aveline ran after her into the wild night.

Suddenly she realized where Primrose was taking her.

To the last place she wanted to go.

"Goodnight, Diary, sweet dreams."
P.P.

Chapter 11

No Place to Hide

Primrose stood by the boy scarecrow, her hands tucked in the side pockets of her parka. Drawing one pale hand out, she beckoned Aveline towards it. Despite her fear of the twisted figure that had haunted her thoughts since she'd first seen it, Aveline knew she had no choice and quickly jumped over the garden wall.

Crouching down, she glanced up at the scarecrow with its demented grin. It loomed above her, rain streaming down its crude, lifeless face, so it almost appeared to be crying. Reaching out, Aveline grasped its coarse sleeve and tugged it towards her, grimacing as she did so. For a second it wobbled precariously, and Aveline shut her eyes, expecting it to topple onto her, but it settled itself, still upright. Now it hid her, just about.

Pull your feet in.

The voice could have been Primrose's, or it might simply have been inside her head, but Aveline obeyed it nonetheless and huddled deeper beneath the embrace of her creepy accomplice. She became aware that Primrose had come to sit beside her.

"You be quiet now. As quiet as the grave," Primrose whispered.

While she feared whatever had been trying to get into the house, Aveline didn't feel at all alarmed by Primrose's presence, which was odd considering she was a ghost, too. Instead she felt comforted. What's more, Primrose had once been in this exact situation herself. There wasn't anyone better to have at her side. Glancing down at Primrose's pale hand, Aveline wondered what would happen if she tried to hold it. Would her hand pass straight through Primrose's? All the ghosts she'd read about had that kind of transparent quality to them, as if a cloud of mist had been made into the shape of a person. But Primrose looked solid enough. She couldn't be sure, but she also thought she could see the rise and fall of Primrose's chest, the girl's breaths a little panicked and ragged, just like her own.

Suddenly, Primrose stiffened.

"She's coming," Primrose said, her words a whisper on the night air.

For a moment, Aveline lost the feeling in her limbs. Her lungs refused to expand. Her heart refused to beat. Fear gripped her in an iron fist.

And over the din of the storm, she heard footsteps.

Not the panicked dash of someone trying to get out of the storm and home to a warm house.

Slow, measured steps, slapping in the water.

Someone searching.

Hunting.

Squeezing her eyes tightly shut, Aveline concentrated on making herself as small and as quiet as possible. In her head, she urged herself to be brave. She regretted leaving the house without a word. Her aunt would be beside herself with worry. She thought of her mum and wished she wasn't so far away. And Aveline wondered whether she'd soon become like Primrose – here, but not here.

And all the while, the footsteps came closer, until Aveline had to resist the urge to run screaming to the cottage door.

Then the footsteps stopped.

Nails scraped along the top of the stone wall.

The smell of brine and dank rock pools washed over them. Unable to keep her eyes shut a moment longer, Aveline glanced up.

A white hand stretched overhead, merely centimetres away. A tangle of seaweed hung from spiny fingers, the nails splintered like shards of black glass. The hand opened and closed, as if it was breathing.

Or sniffing.

Claw-like, the fingers tried to grip the head of the scarecrow, slipping on its smooth, wet surface. The hand drew back, then tried again, softer this time, letting its nails slide slowly down the plastic face as it searched for something to cling to.

And then, for one awful moment, a pale face loomed into view. The skin was cracked like the surface of an antique vase. Bedraggled strands of the blackest hair hung down like creepers, concealing parts of Cora Poole's face but not all. Aveline stifled a whimper. Because where there should have been eyes, all she could see were deep, bottomless black holes.

Next came a rasping breath, like a pebble rattling in a dry throat.

Holding her breath until her chest ached, Aveline remained as rigid as the human statues she'd seen, who stood frozen on a plinth with a bucket for loose change placed in front of them.

I'm not going to let her take me.

In her mind she repeated it over and over again, all the while resisting the urge to cry out as those terrible fingernails scrabbled frantically over the surface of the scarecrow's plastic face, raking it with confused fury.

Suddenly, the hand snatched itself back as if burned, then it flew at lightning speed, swatting the scarecrow's head clean off its shoulders. It rolled through the wet grass before coming to a halt on the path, where it leered back at Aveline as if this was all part of some hilarious joke.

The shock of seeing the disembodied head made Aveline gasp.

The tiniest breath. Nothing compared to the whirling roar of the storm. Yet loud enough to be heard.

Instantly, she covered her mouth.

Too late.

A gleeful shriek echoed through the night, causing what seemed like every dog in Malmouth to start barking. Then those long fingers scuttled back over the wall like some terrible spider, before reaching down to caress the hairs on Aveline's head. Their coldness spread through her skull, down into her jaw and then down further still, until her entire body stiffened.

Like a corpse.

"You leave her alone, Cora, she won't be coming with you tonight."

In the shock, Aveline had all but forgotten that Primrose sat beside her. Now the girl got to her feet and, for the first time, she drew back her hood. Primrose looked pale, but her black eyes shone and a fragile smile played on her blue lips as she stared defiantly at Cora Poole.

"Don't worry, Aveline, you're not going anywhere while I'm here."

As feeling and warmth rushed back into Aveline's body, a triumphant screech made her ears ring. Jumping to her feet, she saw Cora had grabbed Primrose and was now dragging her down the beach towards the frothing sea.

It was happening again, just like it had all those years ago.

Cora Poole taking Primrose off to a watery grave. Only this time it was all Aveline's fault.

And she couldn't stand it.

Aveline jumped over the garden wall and sprinted towards the beach where the pair of them struggled like a black whirlwind. It was impossible to tell one from the other, so Aveline crept nearer, waiting for the right moment. The wind roared in from offshore to push her back with invisible hands, but she bowed her head and took another step towards the desperate struggle.

"Primrose!" Aveline cried. "Give me your hand!"

"No!" Primrose yelled. "Don't come any closer!"

Aveline caught sight of Primrose's face, her features locked into a determined grimace as she grappled with the flailing, ragged figure of Cora Poole. With one almighty heave, Primrose tried to rip herself free of Cora's grip, but a thin skeletal hand gripped Primrose's as tightly as a vice, black fingernails digging into pale flesh.

"Run!" Primrose screamed again. "Leave her to me!"

Aveline hesitated. She knew that Primrose was trying to save her. But as much as she wanted to get far away from the grim shade that had once been Cora Poole, she didn't want to leave alone. If she could only free Primrose, then perhaps the girl might be able to live again? To return from wherever it was that Cora had taken her all those years ago.

Yet, a second later, Aveline knew that delaying had been a mistake.

Possibly the last one she would ever make.

Cora's hand shot out and dug into her wrist like an icy fishing hook. She felt the sting of brine in her eyes, the taste of something fishy and rotten on her lips, and that paralysing sensation of cold – a deeper more penetrating cold than she'd ever thought possible. Digging her feet deep into the shingle, Aveline fought to anchor herself on shore, but the limpet-like grip on her wrist dragged her forward, a cruel pincer that deadened all the feeling in her arm and drained her spirits. The black waves came closer, roaring now as if eager to swallow all three of them up. Aveline tugged again, sensing that Primrose was trying with all her might to help her get free, yet Cora Poole marched on, eager to return to the sea with her prize, two new daughters to replace the ones she'd lost.

Aveline felt her thoughts drift. She felt sad at not being able to say goodbye. Guilty that her mum and family might not ever know what had happened to her. Her body sagged, her grip on Primrose weakened, and she felt her knees buckle.

And Cora Poole laughed, a joyless chuckle of dark desire.

Then Aveline saw a light in the dark.

A torch, cutting through the night like a long golden sword.

"Hey, what's going on down there?"

The crunch of footsteps running through the shingle. A shock of hair made crazy by the whirling wind. And then warmth, beautiful warmth, as Harold reached out and grabbed her by the arm. Strength and courage surged into Aveline's limbs. Her mind cleared and in a single movement she tore herself free from Cora's flailing fingers, falling back onto hard pebbles. Aveline heard a splash as Cora and Primrose entered the water and she tried to get to her feet again, to launch one more desperate attempt to free Primrose, but Harold hugged her to him.

Cora Poole stood at the water's edge, one hand still latched onto Primrose, and turned to stare at Aveline. Her mouth opened and she moaned, and in it Aveline heard the desperation of a lost soul. She took a step towards Aveline and stretched out her other hand, as if silently pleading for Aveline to take it. Only now it was Primrose who yanked Cora back towards the sea, their roles reversed. In the same instant, Primrose's eyes locked onto Aveline's and she saw the girl with the choppy hair mouth one unmistakeable word.

Run!

Then, locked into their final embrace, they disappeared beneath the black waves.

"Primrose!" Aveline cried.

But her only answer was the pounding surf on the shore.

Harold helped Aveline to her feet and together they stumbled back towards the safety of the path. Aveline looked at Harold, his wet hair plastered to his face, and could see only fear, his eyes wide with shock and confusion.

"What was that all about?" he gasped. "It looked like someone was dragging you into the water."

Aveline didn't have the strength to reply.

Cora Poole had gone. She was safe. But Primrose had gone, too, which made her want to cry out in anger and grief. In a short time, she'd made and lost a friend. Her only comfort while fleeing Cora Poole had been knowing she wasn't alone, that Primrose had come to help. Part of her had also hoped to find some way of bringing Primrose back from whatever cold place the lady in the waves had taken her to. But finally she had to accept that her friend had gone.

Maybe for ever.

Pulling off his rain jacket, Harold draped it around her shoulders. "Here, put this on."

"Harold, where did you come from? Did you see… anyone?" Aveline stammered.

"I heard something, but I don't know what exactly – this storm makes everything sound peculiar," Harold said hastily, though Aveline noticed how his hands shook as he used the torch to guide them back towards Aunt Lilian's house. "And then I saw you at the water's edge, looking like you were about to go for a swim, only…there was this strange black fog wrapped around you. It was really weird."

"What are you doing here anyway?" Aveline said. "I thought you said you were staying home?"

"Oh, I just thought it'd be cool to take a walk out in the storm, you know, see how high the waves were," he said, a little evasively. "What were *you* doing out here?"

Aveline shook her head and sniffed. "I was with a friend, she was trying to help me."

She didn't have the energy to tell Harold everything right now, and although he screwed up his face, he didn't ask any more questions.

As they approached the house, an ashen-faced Aunt Lilian ran down the road to greet them, folding Aveline up in the tightest of hugs.

"Oh, Aveline, thank goodness. When I finally got the lights working I came back up and you were gone. I've been searching high and low for you, I thought you were hiding in a cupboard somewhere. What are you and Harold doing out here in this horrible storm?"

Aveline and Harold exchanged a nervous glance, but neither of them offered an explanation and thankfully Aunt Lilian seemed more concerned with getting them out of the rain.

After guiding Aveline gently back to the house, Aunt Lilian made her and Harold sit in front of the fire and wrapped towels around their shoulders, before going off to make them some hot chocolate.

"It was her, wasn't it?" Harold whispered, staring at the floor as if unwilling to see Aveline's reaction. "Cora Poole."

"Yes," Aveline replied, without hesitation. "I couldn't make the scarecrow in time, but Primrose came to help me."

"Primrose?" Now Harold did stare. "Primrose Penberthy?"

Aveline smiled to herself. "Yes," she said quietly. "She saved me."

"Harold," Aunt Lilian said, coming in with a steaming tray of cocoa. "I've called your uncle and he's coming to pick you up in a minute. I'll leave you to explain why you're wet through."

As promised, Mr Lieberman arrived shortly after. Aveline saw her aunt whisper something to him by the doorway, before she led him in.

"Thank you for looking after this drenched rascal, Lilian," Mr Lieberman said. "I'll get him home and into a warm bed. Aveline, I suspect you'll be wanting to do the same."

Once they'd gone, and Aveline had dried out a bit, Aunt Lilian crouched in front of her.

"What happened? When I came back up, the doors were all open and the house was filled with the most pungent smell of seaweed. It smelled like a group of fishmongers had just finished having a meeting."

Aveline couldn't help but laugh. Wiping her nose, she told her aunt all that had happened. Or what she *thought* had happened. She didn't even stop to worry whether Aunt Lilian would believe her. It was the truth, after all. But her aunt didn't interrupt, or question her, or even raise her eyebrows.

"You know Primrose isn't really gone, don't you?" she said at last, once Aveline had finished. "You may not be able to see her any more, but you'll think about her and remember her and that's what really matters. I'm sorry I ever doubted you."

Aveline nodded, nudging a tear away with her knuckle. "That's okay."

"You know, how about this, Aveline? Your mother will be here in a couple of days. Let's agree to no more talk of ghosts or scarecrows. No scary books. Let's lead very boring, ordinary lives for a while, and drink hot chocolate, and eat fish and chips, and watch films. We'll go to bed early and sleep late, and snooze on the sofa in the afternoons in front of the fire. How does that all sound?"

"Um…perfect?" Aveline replied, feeling a grin spread across her face and up to her ears. An odd sensation. It didn't feel like she'd properly smiled for a long time.

Inevitably, after all that had happened, the smile was followed by a yawn, and a stretch, and then another yawn, and before she knew it, Aunt Lilian took her up to her bedroom.

"I would tuck you in, Aveline, but I don't want to put you off coming again."

Outside the storm began to blow itself out, the clouds outside her window breaking apart, through which the occasional star could be seen.

The winds died, the rain stopped, and all that remained was the soft lullaby of the waves.

* * *

Aunt Lilian made good on her promise and the days that followed were full of nothing much and that suited Aveline just fine. Mr Lieberman and Harold came to the house and together they retrieved the books from the attic for his bookshop.

"Ach, there are some real treasures in here," Mr Lieberman said as they sat in the living room and catalogued them.

"Aveline doesn't want them, she only likes weirdo books," Harold said.

"You should stick to eating chips," Aveline replied, sticking her tongue out and getting a grin back from the boy she was beginning to think of as a good friend. Once you got past the stupid haircut and the rudeness, he was actually okay.

Later, Aveline told them *all* about the events of that stormy Halloween night, though her memory of it was increasingly hazy and muddled, the same way a dream drifts away not long after waking. Like Aunt Lilian, they listened, but didn't pass comment. It didn't seem like anybody wanted to talk at length about what had happened. Almost as if they'd made an unspoken vow or pact.

A secret never to be told.

Her mum called the next morning to say she was on

her way and arrived (right on time, much to Aunt Lilian's satisfaction) bursting with a happiness that none of them could resist. Granny was much better, she said, so they could all relax.

After deciding to stay on for the remainder of half-term, their time together passed in a haze of sweet treats and huge meals. Feet were pushed into warm slippers in front of the fire, and the smell of roast dinners and baked puddings made the air smell rich and festive. When the weather stayed kind, they would take a walk on the beach. With the scarecrows all gone, the town lost its sinister atmosphere and became a more pleasant place to be. Occasionally, Aveline's thoughts drifted to Primrose. There hadn't been any odd occurrences in the house since Halloween. During a moment when they were alone, Aveline asked Aunt Lilian if she thought Primrose was still in the house.

"You know, Aveline, I don't. I think Primrose is at peace, don't you?"

Which made Aveline feel both happy and sad.

But Aunt Lilian hadn't got it *quite* right.

It seemed Primrose had one more thing left to do.

A promise to make good on.

On the day they left, Aveline woke to find a pair of red Dr. Martens boots at the bottom of the bed. They hadn't been there when she went to sleep, and there was only one person who would have brought them. But the thought of Primrose being in her room didn't scare her. It was, after all, Primrose's bedroom, too. Gleefully she tried them on and found that they fitted perfectly. She would tell her mum that she'd got them from a charity shop with the money she'd been given. Easy was better than truthful on this occasion.

Once her suitcase was all packed up again, and while Aunt Lilian and her mum talked, Aveline sneaked upstairs and retrieved Primrose's diary. Opening it, she took a pen and wrote in it.

Bye, Primrose, thanks for the boots. I love them. Aveline X

Then she tucked it away in her luggage.

Downstairs, Aveline hugged Aunt Lilian tightly, pushing her face against the warmth of her aunt's cardigan.

"Don't you dare be a stranger, Aveline, or I'll come up to Bristol and fetch you myself."

"I won't, I promise."

Mr Lieberman and Harold arrived a few minutes later, loaded down with an armful of books.

"It's a long drive back to Bristol, Aveline, I think you're going to need some reading material," Mr Lieberman said.

"Thank you."

Lowering his voice, Harold nudged her in the ribs. "I sneaked a few ghost ones in there, but don't tell your aunt, she'll give me extra lessons."

"It'll be our secret," Aveline said. "As long as you stop calling me a weirdo."

"I'll see what I can do. How about Ghost Girl instead?"

"How about Book Boy?"

"Ghost Girl and Book Boy. I like it. We sound like superheroes."

Reaching out, Aveline gave him the briefest of hugs, which he seemed to like, as he quickly hid behind his fringe.

"Anything else strange happens, give me a call," Harold said, handing her a slip of paper with a phone number on it.

"Will do, I promise."

"Come on then, love, let's get going," her mum said.

214

Her mum's voice brought her back into the present. Waving madly to them all, Aveline settled into the car seat, feeling a mixture of relief and regret. As their car turned onto the beach road, Aveline touched her mum's arm.

"Could you stop here a second, Mum? I've just got to do something."

Aveline's mum frowned, but pulled the car to a stop. Opening the door, Aveline ran down to the water's edge. Dark clouds bloomed like black flowers, but the rain was yet to come. A stiff breeze blew off the water, tangy with salt.

Kneeling among the pebbles, Aveline opened her backpack and took out Primrose's diary. She'd made the decision earlier that day. If the police did eventually call, she would simply say that she'd lost it.

Which wasn't really a lie.

She knew what had happened to Primrose, but there was no way the police would ever believe it.

She waited for the next wave to come rushing up over the shingle, before gently placing the diary in the water.

Then she watched the retreating tide carry it away.

Looking across to the harbour wall, Aveline saw a small girl with a rather severe haircut watching her. The girl raised her hand and waved. Aveline waved back, before running back to the warmth of the car. The journey home would be long, boring and completely uneventful.

Aveline couldn't wait to get started.

The End

Acknowledgements

A book is never truly written by one person. While I may have been the one that typed the words, this book was first written by my mum, who used to read to us by lamplight in our cold, dark house in Rochdale. By my dad, who first took me through the wardrobe and into Narnia. By wonderful teachers, Mr Armstrong & Mr Henderson. Those friends I've made along the way (you know who you are) who had the grace to spare a kind word. To Kendal Muse and Jennifer Ray who spared valuable writing time to read an earlier draft, your suggestions were gratefully received. And thanks to Bayo & bigohcoaching.com for the coaching when the going got tough. I'm eternally indebted to Madeleine Milburn, whose godlike finger first plucked this tale from the slush pile, dusted it off, and thus changed my life. Also, thanks to my agent, Chloe Seager, for the ongoing support and all the fantastic team @MMLitAgency. To the astonishing bibliophiles at Usborne – *this* book certainly wouldn't be this book without the incredible guidance of editors Rebecca Hill and Stephanie King, who drew this story out from the shadows. Blessings for the brilliantly uncanny illustrations, Keith. And without the passionate support of Kat and Stevie, this book may not be in your hand right now. To my life partner, Janna, who supplies love and support, ideas and inspiration, I would be lost without you. Finally, to the countless other authors whose voices have yet to be heard – keep going, your time will come.

Meet the Author

I grew up near Manchester, UK, in a house that overlooked a graveyard. It explains a lot, I think. I was always afraid of the dark and reading scary books last thing at night didn't help much either. I would often find myself too afraid to shut my eyes but too scared to keep them open. But that feeling was also one I came to love. Does that sound like you? As a child I particularly liked the authors Alan Garner and Susan Cooper. They made me believe that extraordinary things could happen to ordinary children, and that's part of the inspiration for Aveline's spooky adventures. I was also very aware of landscape and seasons in these books, which is again, something I've tried to emulate here.

I've been lucky enough to live in the UK, Ireland and New Zealand, which are all wonderful in their own way.

These days I live in the Pacific Northwest of America, together with my wife and a grumpy old rescue dog called Lucky. It's misty, rainy and smells of pine. At night, we sleep in a cabin and listen to the coyotes yip-yapping outside. Sometimes there's scratching in the walls, and one autumn evening I heard rustling in the leaves right outside the door. It sounded like footsteps even though there was nobody there. But that was just my imagination, right?

Enough about me. Thank you so much for reading this book, I hope you enjoyed it.

Phil Hickes

Book Club Questions

- Primrose writes, "I live in a place where it's always dark and the wind never stops blowing." Why do you think the author, Phil Hickes, chose this kind of weather for Malmouth? How does he use weather throughout the book?

- While she's staying with her aunt, Aveline doesn't have any phone signal, and can only use the computer for half an hour a day. How do you think this story might be different if Aveline could use more technology?

- "If the roles were reversed, and it was she who'd gone missing, Aveline would be more than happy for Primrose to read her diary." Do you agree with Aveline on this?

- There are lots of different types of writing included in this book, including a book of ghost stories, diary entries and newspaper articles. How do these help the author to tell Aveline's story? Which do you think is the scariest?

- There are illustrations, by the artist Keith Robinson, dotted throughout the book. Pick your favourite. How do you think it helps add to the atmosphere of the story?
- Aveline feels very connected to Primrose, even though she went missing before Aveline was born. What are some of the similarities between the two girls?
- Aveline and Primrose don't just see the ghosts they encounter – they hear, smell and feel strange things as well. Think of some examples from the story. How does the use of the senses make things more spooky?
- Would you put up a child-scarecrow to try to ward off the Lady in the Waves? Think of a design for one, and consider what materials you would use to make it.
- There are lots of legends in *Ghosts and Phantoms of Dorset, Devon and Cornwall* that we don't hear about in this book. Pick one of the titles from the contents on pages 51 and 52, and imagine what the spooky story behind it might be.

Turn on your torches and join
Aveline Jones in her next adventure

Aveline is thrilled when she discovers that the holiday cottage her mum has rented for the summer is beside a stone circle. Thousands of years old, the local villagers refer to the ancient structure as the Witch Stones, and Aveline cannot wait to learn more about them.

Then Aveline meets Hazel. Impossibly cool, mysterious yet friendly, Aveline soon falls under Hazel's spell. In fact, Hazel is quite unlike anyone Aveline has ever met before, but she can't work out why.

Will Aveline discover the truth about Hazel, before it's too late?

Find out in
The Bewitching of Aveline Jones
OUT NOW